Born in 1966 in East Kilbride, **David Cameron** has worked in a residential school for children suffering from epilepsy. David now lives in North Queensferry, in the shadow of the Forth Bridge. A writer of poetry from a young age, his work has been well received by several distinguished poets. This is his first pubished work of fiction.

eau Moon

www.11-9.co.uk

Rousseau Moon

David Cameron

First published by

303a The Pentagon Centre
36 Washington Street
GLASGOW
G3 8AZ
Tel: 0141-204-1109
Fax: 0141-221-5363
E-mail: info@nwp.sol.co.uk
http://www.11-9.co.uk

A catalogue record for this
book is available from the
British Library.

11:9 is funded by the Scottish Arts
Council National Lottery Fund.

ISBN 1-903238-15-3

Typeset in Utopia
Designed by Mark Blackadder

Printed by WS Bookwell, Finland

For Louise

for writing from
Sarsfield Quay
that February

Acknowledgements

Rousseau Moon contains an extract from Salvador Dalí's *A Feather* (La Gaceta Literaria, 1929): © Kingdom of Spain, universal heir of Salvador Dalí, 2000.
© Gala-Salvador Dalí Foundation, by appointment of the Kingdom of Spain, 2000.

Rousseau Moon also contains the first two lines of *Chamber Music V* reproduced with the permission of the estate of James Joyce; copyright © Estate of James Joyce

Peaches and Monkeys' Tails contains an extract from *Peaches* by the Stranglers, © Cornwell, Burnel, Greenfield, Black. Reproduced with the kind permission of Complete Music Ltd.

The Mirror contains extracts from *The Bhagavad Gita*, © Juan Mascaró (translator), London 1962, pp.54 and 67. Reproduced by permission of Penguin Books Ltd.

The Mirror also contains words by Bob Dylan, taken from the song *She Belongs to Me* by kind permission of Special Rider Music – Sony ATV Music Publishing.

• • • • • • • • • • • • • • • • •

The author was awarded a Writer's Bursary by the Scottish Arts Council in February 2000, for which he is grateful.

Contents

The bridge trembles.
Step lightly,
my brothers.

Iain MacDonald,
The Scream

Rousseau Moon

1

Every time I think of this woman who read to us so patiently I see a blue guitar book that had a picture inside it of somebody I call *my Indian maiden*. I did a charcoal drawing of the picture years later, when I met somebody else who looked like it, and photograsphed the drawing over and over, making a montage out of the photographs and other things I'd done. You could say that the picture meant something to me.

She sat on the edge of her table, legs hidden under a cotton dress, reading a John Steinbeck book. Nobody else had read a whole book to us since we were children. She even put on a dumb drawl for the big farm-hand, Lennie. In *Of Mice and Men* Lennie ends up breaking a woman's neck and being shot for it by his friend George. I've never gone back to the book. I think it would only summon the feeling of afternoon in that classroom. The teacher's lulling voice, her dark hair tied in two ponytails, and the thick red lipstick she wore: I can summon these things without it.

We were close to the end of the book one day when her voice stopped suddenly and whispering started up. She called out my name and I asked 'What?' vaguely – I was determined to seem vague.

'What are you wearing in your hair?'

'It's a ribbon,' I answered.

'Yes, it's a red ribbon. I meant, why?'

I explained that I wore the ribbon for a bet.

'I don't mind,' she said. 'I just want to know what it means.' She turned to Ziggy, but Ziggy looked a picture of innocence, amazingly, and said she knew nothing about it.

After the bell, when we were moving outside, she seemed to give up trying to penetrate my secret. Ziggy was standing in the doorway and we let everybody go by. I took the ribbon off and dangled it in front of her, saying in a sing-song voice: 'Red ribbon, red ribbon.' She took it from me and began tying it seductively round her hair. I asked for the money.

'Don't worry, it's yours.'

'This is where you kiss me on the nose and say you're proud of me,' I said.

'It takes more than this, baby. There. It looks better on me.'

I could tell that she was happy with me, so that it hurt when she said she wanted to find Árab.

2

Árab was at home, hiding from his mother. I watched her go past the school gate, her work's overall showing under a camel-hair coat. I was standing back from a group of boys and one girl who were smoking in a circle at the gate, the girl blowing smoke into the mouth of one of the boys. Árab's mother scowled and must have looked only in her direction, or else I was swallowed up in smoke, because she didn't see me.

She disappeared into an underpass and emerged on the other side. I can imagine her arriving home and collapsing on the big brown sofa in the living room. She gets up, puts the ironing away. Árab's eyes are wide as she opens the cupboard door. She literally faints onto the bed, and Árab walks out and stands over her.

3

There was an old black and white photograph on my wall of my Aunt Bea (actually my great-aunt) standing outside a phone-box. She had died when I was three in the room next to mine – the room that my gran, her sister, now slept in.

Árab and I had made a kind of icon out of this photograph; we had made an icon of death.

There were others: a gnarled branch that I carved into a walking-stick and called Medicine-stick; a huge green-handled clasp-knife; a painting by Rousseau, *Carnival Evening*; and our own painting in which we saw a Madonna with wire mesh across her face. There were pylons and telegraph poles that were part of the landscape of the glen and therefore belonged to us. So we believed.

We went down the glen that night. I have the feeling that Árab's mother must have kept quiet about him not being at school, or else his dad just wanted him out of his sight, but anyway we went down, Árab told me about the cupboard incident and we laughed. I told him about registration class, where we were asked what our fathers did. When I said that mine was dead somebody else said: 'He went off to America with his bird.' We talked about the person who said this. Árab shook his head a lot – it really troubled him, which impressed me.

Turning a sort of corner made out of a muck-slope, we saw a gypsy through a gap in the trees – a tinker, Árab called him – on the opposite bank of the river. It was the first time we'd seen him, and he was with the white horse we knew from a different part of the glen. He was wiping clean a metal cup and a plate, with grass.

4

'A feather that is no feather but a tiny herb, representing a sea-horse, my gums on the hill and at the same time a beautiful spring landscape.'

I asked Árab to say it again.

We were talking about Salvador Dalí, and Árab quoted those words. I hadn't known that Dalí wrote poetry. I was more surprised that Árab could quote some to me – it was the only time I ever heard him quote anything.

'A feather that is no feather but a tiny herb, representing a sea-horse, my gums on the hill and at the same time a beautiful spring landscape.' Árab had read that this meant nothing. For me, everything had meaning.

'I think that feather is a pun on father,' I said, since the word 'father' was still fresh in my head.

'Even though it was written in Spanish?'

'It's unimportant, he knew English.'

'You're wrong already,' Árab said, very happy now.

'Dalí is the son wanting to possess the mother. A *father* that is no father, but a tiny herb. He's the tiny herb that's supplanted the father's place.'

'You mean, little Herbie?'

'He mentions the sea-horse because it's the only creature where the male gives birth.' I thought for a second, then spat out the rest. 'The beautiful landscape is his beautiful mother. And my gums on the hill is him as a baby at her breast.'

5

I wasn't always this clever. I didn't notice, for one thing, Ziggy growing close to Árab. What makes things worse is that I believed in warning signs. I watched out for them.

Árab's father taught and my mother worked in our school, so we had to find a realm away from them. We didn't see it like that, of course, but the glen was the place we found.

When I first knew Árab he liked to talk in the science class, in a corner that we shared with two girls, about blowing up the bridges there. Árab hated any sign of man in his beloved glen. A wooden bridge was being erected over the river and he wanted to blow it up. It seemed childish to me, and wrong, and so we argued about it. Árab was good at taking arguments to a surreal place where I couldn't win. I remember asking, 'What about blind people, they might use the bridge?' Even the girls were laughing at me.

'You wouldn't think like that if you went down there for yourself,' he said. 'You don't even begin to understand.'

I had been to the glen years before. I remembered tadpoles moving like sperm in dark water. It was more a stench in the nostrils than the mystical place Árab spoke of.

I said something cocky like this in reply, but I felt he was right. I felt like a small fool suddenly.

6

There were six children outside my house playing fivestones. I couldn't yet have been carrying Medicine-stick, or I would remember. Probably my clothes had degenerated and I was wearing the torn wine-dark jumper and oil-stained jeans. Tearing was a magical operation. One thing I couldn't bring myself to do was write on my clothes as Ziggy did. I hated that.

I made my way to Árab's through the old part of town. I was able to see the unimaginative dark blue flats as Chinese shacks, huddled on top of one another.

Árab had been talking all week about Aztecs and hallucinogens, telling me that it was the season for magic mushrooms to appear. Last September he had eaten some. This was June, though, but he was adamant that some rogue mushrooms might be out. It was seven months since the first night in the glen, the first night we both went down there. I had gone to prove him wrong, of course. Now I was as dedicated to wildness as he was.

Nobody answered the door when I got to his house, and I found him round the back with his father. They were burning old wood and stuff out of the shed. It was as if his father signalled invisibly for him to go when I appeared, but for once I wasn't anxious to leave, until Árab's grin made me remember the mushrooms.

The space between Árab's house and the glen was

strange. It took ten minutes to walk it, if you went the quickest way. It was mostly one long road going uphill. A line by Robert Frost, 'Or highway where the slow wheel pours the sand', makes me think of it.

We were at the last island of houses before the glen and for some reason were hesitant about entering. I sat on a stone bollard while Árab sprawled out on the grassy path at my feet. We were smoking and saying the first things that came into our heads. Árab snorted with pleasure as he turned his hand in the air. He was looking intently at an insect that was crawling on him. It was a red spider – that was the name we both knew it by.

Then there were the two paths into the glen. We didn't take the path of the first night, but the ordinary one, which opened onto the fields where the mushrooms would be.

We went up the steep slope of the hill that was almost unwalkable, and I followed a winding strand of reddish mud to the top. It seems to me now that the fields at the top there, beyond the wire, could have been Árab's favourite part of the glen. There were telegraph poles spread far apart, very plain ones, which we called Dalí crutches. We played with the thought that they held up the sky, like the crutches in Dalí's painting holding up the image of Sleep. The bareness of the land here and the simplicity of the details meant that it was hard to think of it as surreal. It's why calling the telegraph poles crutches gave us pleasure.

I knew vaguely what I was looking for – small mushrooms with a nipple peak – but it was clear that there were none, and we ended up simply dragging what wood we could gather, mainly branches that we had to jump on to snap, and some clumps of dry grass and twigs that were close to us, and built a fire. It was beginning to get dark, a dark blue anyway, and there would be no warden about to prevent us. 'We could be over there,' I said, looking at a spot diagonally across from us, where the fence intersected the river. 'We could be there looking back at ourselves sitting at the fire.'

A few seconds later we were running across the field. It might have been comic, the sight of our bodies lurching across uneven ground, except that we were serious. Even our laughter when we got there was serious.

We were smiling like children, staring at our own absence.

'Let's leave the fire like that,' Árab said. We walked, not back through the wood, but over the hill towards the rugby pitch and the Golf Club and onto the road. It was the long route back to Árab's. Our thoughts grew more ordinary with hard tarmac under our feet.

No, I *was* carrying the stick that got called Medicine-stick and I was dressed in my harlequin clothes, the bleached-white jeans and jumper that was too big for me. I never remember what Árab wore outside school, not anything scruffy though. I might have looked outlandish, I'm not certain, but as we reached the first houses from the glen a man appeared, walked quickly towards us and said: 'What do you two do down there? There's something not right about the two of you.' He said some more, and I could see that we frightened him.

Árab's eyes narrowed with hatred. 'You fucking old man,' he said. 'You fucking stupid old man.'

7

It was the next day that I got home. My mother was emptying brown water out of the green jug she used for a vase. It wasn't difficult, from her worried look, to work out that somebody was coming.

My mother's cousin's niece had died, and this cousin and another woman came with the child's grandfather. He was very drunk, a heavy, large Irishman with a black overcoat and a hand that wandered over his face. I was manoeuvred into the kitchen and told to keep back from him.

He hung between the two women as though they were crutches. The object was to feed him whisky and cake until he left, but he insisted on talking, to an apparition in the centre of the room it seemed, and flapping the folds of his coat.

I learned from him that my grandfather had written poetry. He tried to remember some, couldn't, and quoted Keats instead.

The rest of the afternoon was the same thing over and over.

I grew tired of the old man, and washing the cups later I narrowed my eyes to make things intense and vivid again. I thought of Ziggy's coat with its paisley-pattern shapes like embryos or tears. It became mixed up with the dead girl and I thought of a phrase – nightingale tears – that I might be able to use sometime.

8

Architecture does not matter, in one sense. Anyone going through my home-town would hate it unless they wanted to move there to bring up children. Where Ziggy lived, it was not so bad. It feels now that going to see her couldn't have happened in a new town, but somewhere that requires words such as 'the ancient lake of my heart'; words that give a feeling of dampness in the chest.

I looked forward to the smell of coffee in her room. She wasn't always at the door to meet me, but I wasn't made to wait in another room for her. Not exactly a spiral staircase, the stairs did make you turn round in a short space: a disorientating experience, like the preparation for a ritual. I clumped up them unritually, knocked once – it was more like a brush of the hand – and went in.

Her uniform was still on, and for some reason a wave of disgust went through me. She didn't notice, and looking happy – I was always hanging back, watching – came quickly towards me.

'I've not changed,' she said. 'Do you mind?'

'Of course I don't,' I said.

'I'll change if you want me to.'

'As long as I only have to close my eyes.'

'Who said you have to close them? Well, you do,' she said.

'They're closed.'

'Don't open them.'

She would be changing into her jeans, or sometimes a long skirt. If it was the long skirt she would come over and sit on my knee, be babyish, and I would stroke her legs. Tonight she wore jeans, which meant we would talk.

She went downstairs to make coffee and I looked through her records. With the coffee we smoked two cigarettes. A stick of jasmine was burning next to a postcard of a fisherman. Ziggy told me to put Leonard Cohen on. 'It's what I want to hear tonight,' she said.

Her record player was tiny, a turntable and two speakers each the size of a child's shoe-box. The sound was nearly unimportant: it could as easily have been etched in skin, since what mattered was that it should be real, like the dust which choked the needle, stopping every record before the end.

'I like this one,' she said. It was clear that there was some kind of narrative, which I tried to follow, but contempt for the song made me give up.

'I want more coffee,' I said.

'Listen, shit.'

I began to parody Cohen's singing and I thought Ziggy was parodying it too, but she was genuinely singing.

'I was looking for mushrooms with Árab,' I said. 'If we find some, do you want any?'

'I might.'

'We couldn't take them here.'

'No.'

'You'd have to come down the glen with us.'

'Yes.'

'Would you?'

'Yes.'

'Will you come down with me tomorrow?'

'No.'

Cohen was dissolving into hysterics.

'I was listening to this last night, curled up in a ball,' she said, 'and rocking backwards and forwards. It was an amazing feeling, just so reposed. I thought about you in it too. I could have stayed like that for hours. But then my mum was shouting from the bottom of the stairs. I've never hated her so much.'

Her sister, as though she'd heard, was outside the door, calling her.

'I'm not disturbing anything,' she said, half inside the room. She was beckoning Ziggy outside, with some embarrassment, or the embarrassment was mine: it was a tampon she wanted.

Ziggy's sister's name was Marie. Like Ziggy, she had red hair, only finer and more closely cropped. Perhaps it was her height – she was much taller than either Ziggy or me – but I always felt that she was statuesque somehow. *Breezy* is the other word. Statuesque and breezy: I can't explain the contradiction.

9

The next time I saw Ziggy she said she had a present for me: four kittens that Marie had found abandoned on a moor. They were tortoiseshell, female, and I picked the most frightened-looking. I took her home on a bus in a cardboard box with a square of red fabric over her head. There was a thunderstorm, and a sickly yellow light in the bus. She never took to me, I like to think because of that journey.

I don't know which moor Marie meant. There were

moors which extended from the glen and which we didn't find, since we kept to the same ground usually, two square miles or so, except once in summer when we walked for miles across marshy ground.

I remembered that the word *moors* frightened me as a child.

The cat being there brought Ziggy round more often. She would torment it, wrapping it up in her head-scarf or locking it in the box I kept my poems in. This went on for a month or two until we went back to staying at her place. It's strange that we were only together in Árab's once. She did visit him on her own. Árab's mother was suspicious and could smell the cigarette smoke in his room after Ziggy left. I laughed when I heard she considered Ziggy a bad influence.

The search for mushrooms stopped and became the long wait for them to appear. Ziggy laughed at Árab's description of the nipple peak being big as a thumbnail – he was wrong, or meant it as a joke, and it is possible that Árab hadn't taken them the September before – but she was never with us when we looked for them.

About halfway between my house and Árab's was one entrance to the glen, near the Protestant church, and exactly at the spot where a pylon stood. We met there, this time with Ziggy.

She was wearing a purple scarf I didn't recognise. Árab and I were talking in broken sentences and low voices and laughing at nothing. Ziggy seemed to enjoy herself even more, as if she were listening to learn the rules of a game she knew she'd be expert at. We crossed the river over stepping-stones, some of which Árab had put in place. When *Of Mice and Men* was being read to us I understood the part where Lennie is walking closely in George's footsteps, even in an open space: I caught myself walking behind Árab in the glen like this, watching which stepping-stones he chose. I suppose I was easily led – it amuses me to put it like that.

He was very quick to make it across. Thankfully

Ziggy was more hesitant. We managed to get to the wire fence, which wasn't barbed, and sagged where so many bodies had pushed through. It was open land, half concealed in a fold of the glen close to a main road, and smelled of nettles and electricity.

I was feeling restless even before we got to the depressing spot of black burnt earth that was littered with Dryburgh's cans. There was a car tyre there too and for some reason this sickened me most of all. Ziggy and Árab were content to stand around trailing sticks through the ashes. Árab jammed a stick into one of the cans and held it up, emptying beer out of it and tossing it up high. It was the last straw when I felt some of the beer hit me.

I used to run off in those days and sulk, and it's what I did now, back in the direction of the pylon until I was out of sight. I climbed a tree at the corner of the field. I was breathing hard from the run and the cold air was grating my insides in a way that I liked, that I felt purified me.

I tried to enter a dark poetic mood, but I was too interested in what Ziggy and Árab might be doing or saying. Minutes passed and they hadn't followed me. Then I saw smoke and realized that they had lit a fire. I settled into a fork of the tree, put my collar up, and pretended to sleep.

Eventually they did appear at the far end of the field and walked towards where I was hidden. I thought I should shout something out: they could be doing anything. Such as what? Holding hands, at most.

I waited until they were passing almost under the tree and I was just about to say 'Hello there' as though nothing was wrong when Ziggy glanced up at me. She looked away again and they went on walking. I started to climb down and had to shout after them. Still it was 'Hello there' that came out.

They stopped and waited without turning round, but when I caught up with them Árab looked at me with burning eyes and said: 'Pathetic.' Ziggy smiled a little.

I was content to pick up their stride. Ziggy didn't want to cross the river at the same place, so we moved along up the bank of long grass. There were nettles there and instinctively I glanced round for dock leaves. I didn't see any, but I did see something.

It was paper fluttering in the grass. I wouldn't have looked twice but a photograph caught my eye. 'Naked,' I found myself thinking. I went off the track that Árab and Ziggy were making in front of me to look at it close up. It was wet. The pages tore as I lifted them.

Ziggy and Árab started to turn back. The photographs were in black and white. There were photographs of men without erections, with women's heads at their waists, tongues stuck out.

Ziggy wanted to know how I could even hold the thing, but she took it into her own hands and ripped it up. Árab recovered one of the scraps; I always knew when he was genuinely interested, and he was now: he was rolling his thumb and forefinger just below his nose and sniffing them. He had sided with me for a second. The truth was that all three of us were shaken.

We walked in silence for a few minutes, aimlessly now, until Ziggy spoke. 'Theresa's having a party tonight,' she said, 'she wants you two to come.'

'Do you want to go?' I asked Árab. He said nothing, which meant 'maybe'.

'If we can get some alcohol,' he said.

'That's yes, I take it,' Ziggy said.

10

My brother Stephen was at home, playing my guitar – upside-down, since he was left-handed – and singing one of the songs his friend wrote. He had a strange style of playing that involved bending high notes mostly and a blues sound that didn't quite come off. I walked round gran in the kitchen and managed to make some toast. She threw the knife I'd used to butter it into the sink.

It was late afternoon, Stephen should have been at Art School, I should have been at school.

He sang the chorus twice and the line 'The dried remains had left their stains'. *So you know what that means,* I thought; *so, I do too.*

That night I met Árab at the Kingfisher, a chip shop in the town centre. There were five of us – Ziggy wasn't with us yet – and between us we had enough for a bottle of something.

'Of what?'

'Rum,' I said.

'No, vodka,' Árab said.

Árab recognized somebody walking out of the Kingfisher who took a minute's persuasion to buy the bottle for us.

I didn't drink much, saying 'It's not rum,' but Árab was guzzling it down. 'I can hold my drink,' he said, and pretended to drop the bottle.

Ryan was there. The other two were Spence and Brobyn.

We walked past a security guard at the arcade and Spence started to run; without thinking, we ran with him, looking back to see the guard holding the walkie-talkie to his face. When we got to the mirrored corridor of shops Spence decided to urinate: this time we ran and left him. Nobody picked him up, though, and we met him again outside the tax centre. Ahead of us was a maze of streets, swing parks, roundabouts. I couldn't be sure which street was hers. These were like the streets I knew whose names were all connected to Shakespeare: Hamlet, Othello, Macbeth ... We were semi-drunk and looking up at the street-names. A girl was blow-drying her hair at an open window. Spence sang

Lean out of the window,
Goldenhair.

The window shut with a sound like Tupperware being sealed.

We found the house in the end, after a phone call to Ziggy's that her mother answered. She had the address in front of her. I think I managed not to sound very drunk, except that I was talkative. Something we didn't do as a rule was talk much to parents, our own or others'. Only Ziggy was halfway friendly to her parents.

The sky-blue front door opened before we reached it and Theresa was standing with a bright yellow toy trumpet in her fist. 'We don't have any presents,' I said, thinking *not even a toy trumpet,* and smiled casually. Unexpectedly, she did seem annoyed.

The party was underway, but I felt strange and went into the kitchen for some water. Standing at the kitchen window, I could see the nape of somebody's neck in sunshine. The somebody was Ziggy.

I stood in the back door and watched her. She was kneeling down, stroking a cat with both hands. The evening sunlight was making me feel more sober. I hadn't expected her to look subdued tonight.

'Hello there,' I said, just as I'd done earlier in the day. Ziggy smiled hello back, not looking at me.

'I've been drinking,' I said, before she could accuse me.

'Is Árab with you?'

'In the living room.'

'Drunk?'

'Wasted. He downed half a bottle of vodka. He met somebody outside ...'

'Let's not talk about him,' she said. I thought *All right,* and joined her leaning against the wall.

'He looks nothing like Felice,' she said. Felice was the name she'd given my cat (she was still stroking Theresa's cat). 'You want more from me than you're getting, don't you?' she said.

'I don't know what you mean,' I said, but as soon as I said it I did know.

'I saw the way you were looking at the women in

the magazine.'

'No,' I said, incredulous. 'It was funny.'

'You think so?' She looked up at me.

'I mean, they were so corny.'

'I don't know about corny. It made it look disgusting ... It wouldn't be like that with me and you.'

'Are you serious?'

'Yes, I'm serious. I don't want us to wait. You look shocked.'

'No.'

'You don't want to.'

'I do. I mean, I do.'

'You *are* shocked, aren't you? I thought you wanted.'

'No, I really do. It's just that I didn't expect it.'

'That's good.'

Finally I had said the right thing.

One crow, and then another, landed in the garden. The cat puckered its face and ran at them. Ziggy said to me, tenderly I thought, 'Come here.'

I wasn't in her arms for long, though. Theresa appeared, flushed and almost crying. She wanted me to do something with Árab, who was face down on the living room carpet, vomiting.

'I have to see this,' I said. But seeing Árab, I did begin to worry. There was such a corpse-stare in his face and sick was seeping out of his mouth like water out of somebody drowned.

'They're like thought bubbles,' Spence said, staring at the pools of sick. He drew his lips back and bared his teeth in a grin that was meant to show amusement. I didn't ask him to help carry Árab outside.

Nobody thought of calling a taxi, and I ended up walking Árab, with only Ryan to help me, to a main road. In the confusion of leaving the party suddenly, I had been separated from Ziggy, and she left me with a wistful expression on her face to remember her by. It wasn't wistful, it was pleading and angry, and she refused to join us. Later when I stood with Ryan, with Árab stretched out on the pavement, hailing taxis that wouldn't stop for us, I thought that perhaps Ziggy had meant tonight. Could she have meant tonight? It was the only explanation.

Eventually one taxi-driver did stop without pulling away again. I told him we had no money, but that Árab's father would pay.

'That's this lad here's father?' he said. He looked amused, and held the door open for us as we eased Árab inside. He was a good-humoured man and suddenly I felt that everything would be all right. I pictured his grin on Árab's dad's face, a wry smile for us as we propped up his son on the doorstep and he felt for some change.

I don't remember him paying the taxi. Ryan had left me to confront him alone, but there was no confrontation, and I was dismissed without words. I recognized the look of disgust he turned on Árab: it was, feature for feature, the same face Árab had turned to me earlier that day in the glen. There was some word spoken as the door closed but it was too muffled for me to make out.

11

Árab wasn't at school on Monday: by the end of the week he still hadn't appeared. I couldn't phone. Too many days had passed for me to behave naturally on the phone. Ziggy seemed to contrive to be away from me. There was only one class we were both in, but we sat at opposite ends of the room. She was in a rush to be somewhere whenever the bell went. The replacement teacher – my Indian maiden was off sick – was an ex-football player who was gruff and didn't let us walk about the room, which was how normally I'd get a message to Ziggy: sometimes just innocuous lines from a song, one that we knew the words to, which said 'I love you' in it somewhere.

The deputy head wanted to see me. I thought that maybe I was to represent the school at something, though I hadn't been asked to do this in the last two years, since my dismal failure to identify a husky in a quiz. Outside his office was a painting of St Bridget: it must have been moved there recently. I'd listened to a speech about her, standing beside a long swirling banister looking down at a crowd. It gave me a shock of vertigo to remember. And I'd stood there an age earlier, taken into the school by my mum, and looked up at the painting of the saint. There were purple ribbons in the painting, swirling like the banister – for whatever reason. I must have been about five, and there wasn't any crowd below me, and my brother's name wasn't written in gold lettering on a plaque: 'School Captains'. There was fibreglass in the fire doors. I couldn't remember anything about Bridget.

The door opened and there were the steely blue eyes. I thought for a second he was about to shake my hand, but he wanted past me. I was to step inside while he rushed off somewhere. I didn't make the mistake of sitting in the comfortable chair.

Snatches of the Dylan song about Billy the Kid were playing in my head. It was the word 'deputy', delivered to me on the back of a registration slip, that had started me thinking of the Wild West. The spine of the biggest book I could see said *Atlas* on it, and if I hadn't been paralysed at that moment I would have taken the book down and opened it at North America. He came back in and closed the door. He was one of the élite band of teachers who still wore gowns, though there was no chalkdust on his.

'You're wondering why you're here,' he said. I could see the complete circle of the iris in each of his eyes. I think I made a mirror image of his expression. 'Your spiritual life,' he said. I didn't flinch. He tilted back his head.

If it was my cue to speak, I missed it. He started up again.

'What is it that you believe? ... I'll let you into a secret. Some important people were assembled here recently, in this room, and that was – briefly – the topic of conversation. What is it that we really believe? Margaret, one of the cleaning ladies, knocked on the door. Perhaps you know her. She was a little embarrassed at having interrupted us, but before she could escape, one of my colleagues had put the same question to her, in an offhand way. Margaret said: "I believe in one God, the Father, the Almighty, maker of heaven and earth" – and so on. She put us to shame ... I think I might expect a response to this question. Whom do you read? Again a puzzled expression. I can often tell where somebody is at spiritually by the sort of person he admires, which books, which *particular authors*, he reads, and so on. You see what I am driving at?'

Árab in the glen had brought along a blue book of Blake's poems, for me to read the one with the watchman of the night in it. I heard myself say: 'William Blake.'

'Ah, Blake – a maverick. That tells me a great deal about you. It's the reason I asked you here.'

There was some more, then he got started on my friendship with Árab. So it was about Árab's bad influence on me, all this. He must know about me delivering Árab drunk to his father. But Árab's father was a secretive man and perhaps he didn't know. It didn't matter: the conversation would end and be forgotten. Why hadn't Árab been back?

It was lunch-time now. In five minutes these corridors would be swarming, but I was going ahead of everyone, out of school, down to the centre. I had some money, for food or cigarettes.

Just outside the school gate I felt weak. There was nobody about, so I sat down on the grass verge and waited for my heart to stop pounding. I looked up at a tree that had grown through the concrete slabs and at the sky behind it. The thought came into my head that a tree is a cloud. Perhaps I was getting delirious.

I could smoke my last cigarette here, though it was risky. I was being like my mother, lighting up when I felt anxious. I wasn't to think about that.

'Whom do you read?' His words were splashed over the school landscape like ink. The optimism and confidence that had oozed out of his voice were venom to me. And yet the words were harmless, really. Something about the cadence of them reminded me – of what? A song. *Who Do You Love?* Now I could put a lid on the experience.

I was too lost in thought to notice the cigarette burn down and then I was exasperated with myself. I straightened up. I had to walk quickly.

At the underpass I thought of Árab once more, because we used to smoke here.

There were four paths I could take now and I thought ahead and imagined what I would do as I walked down each one. It sickened me, the fact that my limbs must keep moving, that I would see this there, and that there, and nothing would change me, and I would change nothing. I wanted to be back looking into the cage of boughs and not be crushed by time.

There was the world outside myself, and I woke to meet it every day. Woke from what? That was also an encounter, and growing more strange. Things inside me were slowly collapsing. I couldn't be sure that something else was taking their place. I became very silent to see if I could observe anything there. What if the houses were made of glass? I saw people moving through the rooms. The ones who were seated stood up to shake hands with the ones who had just entered. Nobody saw the people in the other houses through the glass. I could see all this, and it was played out to a very light tinkling music, a Chinese music perhaps, like the sound boats sometimes make in a harbour. There had been times on my way home from Ziggy's, in the patches where the streets were empty, when Medicine-stick had been my elegant cane tapping a monotone so sinister that women cowered in their beds. And then at home, staring at the cracks in the wall in front of me until words came: 'The Venice horn staggers life ... Eyes fixed on one star ... ' They didn't have to make sense, just startle a sleeping part of my brain. The less the wall-shapes resembled something, the better. They had been there even in my childhood, unknown continents and misshapen animal heads, all in a milky sea, which my eyes rowed through. I saw sounds, not words – eerily creaking masts tilted dangerously.

Or I imagined Aunt Bea's coffin suspended above the slant wooden ceiling at home: thirteen years it had been there. None of this satisfied me. True imagining changed – or so it felt – the chemical composition of the body, which helped preserve the corpses of saints. There might be some shining place where I could walk and make peace with my family, but the thought of it only stayed with me until I pictured a cover of *Watchtower* with an American family strolling through boring Eden.

There was something terrifying in the landscape, haunting and terrifying.

12

The presence might have been my twin, but he separated himself from me and was lagging some distance behind. It didn't seem to matter, I was so engrossed by the scene. It was a land torn apart by civil war, but the light and the space made it still beautiful. There was a mass of wire and crumbling white walls, in fact rubble everywhere – I felt it on the soles of my feet. I passed one man who was squatting over something, a small photograph perhaps, pressed into his left palm, and who seemed rooted in the landscape: he had an air of authority. He looked up when I was near but he looked through me. He might have been the gypsy from the glen.

The sky was a tremendous blue that threatened to turn blue-black. I tried to count the domes I could see and wondered if they were temples, but I lost count. The explosions were far enough away to ignore. Out of a hole in the ground, a few feet from me, someone was writhing. I thought for a second I recognized his eyes – I was wrong, the writhing figure was an animal, a lynx in fact. It trotted round the squatting man and they acknowledged one another. Then the earth started to move.

Small stones were rolling along the ground towards me, as if kicked by some other creature, one that I should fear. Without seeing him, I knew suddenly that this was the presence I'd shaken off earlier, and that he was as supple as the lynx. I ran. The ground I ran over looked like it was marked out for some event, but it was the light from a window solidified and lengthened in the dark.

Now I really was running. The landscape of rubble and ash was giving way to a familiar landscape and soon I was running down streets that I knew as though down a tunnel. It was a tunnel in so far as it was leading inexorably to one place.

I was being pursued, not by a presence or a shadow, but a man, and though I didn't look back, I knew he was gripping a kitchen knife and that he would use it on me. The streets were empty. There was a beacon at the corner of Lauder Green, a lighthouse, which made me look down to see if it was water under my feet. The pavement was still there but there were inches of green sea-water. It would be all right, though, because I was nearly home.

Nothing about my street was different or dream-like, and the air was noticeably cooler. I felt that I could slow down now, like an athlete well out in front at the finishing line, but then I realized I would have to knock and wait at the door. Everything depended on how quickly it was answered.

Stephen opened the door, guitar in hand, wearing his school uniform, which I felt should have surprised me. I would work it out later. Inside, my two other brothers Michael and Tom were there, Tom standing at the fire below the porthole-mirror. He looked pleased to see me. Michael had his head turned towards the TV, which didn't appear to be on. He glanced up at me with a hello-look.

I was going to explain everything to them when I remembered that he was still outside. I looked through the blinds. He was there, walking, dressed in black, the fingers of his right hand bunched up – he had hidden the knife in his sleeve.

Now my brothers had to be told quickly. I couldn't speak. I could show them, though. I tried to drag Stephen to the window, but he was only amused by me, and so I gestured despairingly until all three looked at me and I pointed outside. I'd have to continue the dumb show and I ran into the kitchen to get a knife from the drawer. Before I could run back to show them it, though, I hesitated, and saw that the knife in my hand could be my weapon. I didn't need my brothers.

Time slowed down and the living room seemed a world away. The back door wasn't shut right. My hand was on the handle but I didn't want to push it. Against every instinct, I opened the door, and stepped out into the back garden.

The garden was full of dying cattle. I couldn't tell which ones had finished dying – one carcass made a low rumbling cry like a foghorn. Raw flesh was exposed; innards were hanging out. I was surprised to see a calf standing, but it soon toppled over, setting the wire clothes-line vibrating (it made a sound like the bass-string of a guitar). There were even pieces of meat, whole flanks, hanging from the line. All of the cattle were white. I was knee-deep in gore.

Beyond the hedge, in the gravel square, was one other creature I didn't notice at first – a horse, white also, which, though it was immobile, still strained forwards. The one eye that I could see was pointed and mad.

If it was a scene of desolation, still it was a torpid world unthreatened by the man who would murder me. But I stepped out of the gore, back inside, and the panic resumed.

My mind was a tunnel and I was being hurtled towards the light. I crossed the living room past my useless brothers with the knife ready in my hand. I had to tell someone. Was it safe to turn my back to the front door and go up the stairs? On the hallway wall was a faded picture of some rustic scene that couldn't pretend not to be menacing now. Somebody was crazy in the long grass. Somebody was hiding there.

I wasn't running any longer, though the panic hadn't diminished, and I walked up the fourteen stairs to the top landing. The stairs' carpet was from years ago. At the top there was a left- and a right-hand turn. Which room was mine? We had swapped rooms so many times, and mum changed the furniture about almost every month. I went right, telling myself this was *west*.

I didn't even reach the door; I froze as the corner of my eye caught the window that looked onto the back. Everything was the same as it had been; the horse was there, strangled from this perspective by the wires of the telegraph poles.

My time to forget the murderer had run out, the knife was in my hand, and I swivelled round to the two doors on the right. The first was gran's room, I knew that: a stale smell escaped from under the door. Her room was so small, she wouldn't be able to provide a hiding place.

I went into the other room, remembering that it was mine as the door opened. I had to adjust to the room's darkness. What light there was was dark red. In the reddish light – someone, who was it?

Gran was in the room, standing beside the window. She was beside the window holding open the red curtain, at an acute angle so that I couldn't see out. I couldn't see any daylight other than what shone on her. The meaning of this was clear and I perceived it at the same time as I took in the scene. She was conspiring with whatever was outside: the knifeman, if it was him. The held-open curtain was a signal.

She was simultaneously looking outside and looking at me, gauging my reaction. She flickered between being gran and a Janus-statue, like a primitive cartoon, in that red light. I reacted by running out of the room.

I was moving as if underwater, with or without the

knife, towards my mother's bedroom. I knew that everything pointed to this place. Whatever was going to happen, happened here.

13

Mum left for work without bothering me too much; Stephen was at home going back and forth, but he was tolerant of my being there lying in bed, in an older-brother way that I appreciated as I pulled the red and black blanket further over my head.

Someone was at the door, and I heard footsteps coming upstairs. Stephen walked into the room to say that Árab 'and some other clown' were downstairs. I pulled on my jeans and a jumper and went down, feeling nervous about Árab being here, and not emerged yet from my sleepy state. I thought I could get him to leave with an arrangement to meet somewhere. Who was with him? I'd forgotten to speculate. I opened the living room door and saw that it was Spence.

Árab was speaking to Stephen and they were passing the guitar between them, Árab trying to work out the chords Stephen played upside-down. Spence acknowledged my presence. He looked a little bit drunk. I checked the clock: eleven.

I looked at my face in the mirror: my hair was sticking up. When I came back from the kitchen a few seconds later, bath-towel in hand, Stephen had gone. Spence and Árab were almost jumping.

'We've got it,' Árab said with a wide smile. He took a jam jar out of his coat, put it against his cheek and rolled it across his lips. It was filled with brown liquid.

I waited, not asking what it was.

'The mushrooms.'

'What?'

'The mushrooms.'

'How?'

'It's some of my brother's batch from last year,' Spence said. 'Dried out. He had hundreds of them.'

'We made mushroom tea,' Árab said. 'We had ours, this is for you.'

I didn't believe them; then I looked at their eyes.

'What was it like?'

'Amazing, but not as strong as when they're fresh. It lasted what – an hour? Take it now and we'll go down the glen.'

'I'll take it when I get there,' I said.

'No, now, it'll start to work by the time we're there.'

I was afraid, but I kissed the jar, opened it, and drank without breathing. The aftertaste was foul.

'You drank it all,' Árab said.

'Was that wrong?'

'No,' he said, lying. I grew afraid in my stomach.

'I still want to wash,' I said. 'Is that all right?'

Árab shrugged.

I was in the shower for a few minutes and knew I should get out, but the warmth kept me there. I was wiping and showering the mirror to try to see myself through the steam, to see if my face was changing. It felt that it could be. I heard Spence's voice, singing downstairs, with probably Árab playing the guitar.

I'd taken the black showerhead off its perch and was holding it in my hand when it started to interest me. At first it was something grotesque, menacingly black, Nazi-like, but soon it was something else; not exactly a snake, but a creature I had tamed. Once I was out of the shower a pain in my stomach caused me to stretch out on the cold linoleum, something I used to do as a child. I saw that the hand-towel was the one my aunt had brought from holiday – an unusual one, with a scorpion on it, and the word underneath, *schorpeon* I think. There was something amusing about the linoleum that I hadn't noticed before. I said the word 'laburnum'.

Árab was knocking on the door. I said 'All right, all right,' but he went on knocking, softly and mechanically, until half-dressed I opened the door to his grinning face. He was laughing at me laughing, he said. So – I was laughing.

Once I was dressed I had to find my boots. Árab wasn't helping, looking in impossible places and saying, 'They're not here, your boots.' It was funny; but I was growing confused. He seemed to look at me darkly, but the darkness he was conjuring up was out of place with the piles of ironing and the pattern of the carpet. He held up the Rousseau print and told me to describe it. There were two figures holding hands in the clearing of a forest at night; perhaps not a forest. And there was a round moon and a few strangely shaped clouds.

Árab saw a third figure. 'By the bandstand. You can see half of him.'

He seemed to be right. Now there was a sinister element, the shadowy figure that stood, half-hidden and threatening. It was more than half-hidden. I noticed the dust on the glass of the frame, and to break the spell said: 'This is human skin.' Then I escaped into the bedroom where Stephen was and looked soberly for the boots.

Time was dragging on and I couldn't find anything to put on my feet, and my stomach was really churning now. In the kitchen I bent over the blue washing basket in the cupboard under the stairs, stroking Felice. I could see how wise she was. 'Amazing colours,' I said as I looked at her fur: it was like tar streaked with other, orangey colours, but with the feel of silk. She snapped her head round and bit me. I was stroking her harder, determined to make peace, but she jumped out and wriggled round the door. There, next to the door, with a claw hammer inside one of them, were my boots.

'Can we go now?'

I was focused. I needed money: in the sliding-door cupboard in the living room there was usually some silver lying about. I had a strong, overpowering feeling of *déjà vu* as I opened the cupboard door. I found two coins and something that interested me: a bulky watch that I'd been told you could go diving with – theoretically, because the glass in the face was cracked. How had it cracked?

The walk to the glen was underway, without Spence or Árab, without a coat, just myself striding out; but before I'd got to a road they'd caught up with me. It was a warning that I needed protecting. Árab offered to go back for my coat but I wouldn't let him – there were a lot of things I had to talk to him about, which couldn't wait.

I was vaguely afraid of meeting someone who knew me, of the eyes beside curtains looking out, but my stride was unrelenting. It took me to the top of Blackbraes and past the woods nicknamed the Silent. Everything was bathed in a yellow light.

I was talking to Árab about the wheel. The wheels of cars passing astonished me, the motion both fast and still, like bodies dancing in strobe light. The concept of movement had changed and I began to speak about Zeno's Arrow – keep on halving the distance between an arrow and its target, and the target could never be hit – except that it came out, apparently, as Zeno's Sorrow. I stepped onto the road and Árab caught me.

This way was best for avoiding people, but I felt that we were drifting, that this was the wrong direction. It broke on me that it was school I needed to get to. Árab couldn't believe what I was saying. I was doubtful too, though I managed to disguise it: it was a source of pride that I could be deceitful in this state.

I wanted to get to the school so that I could walk into the windowless lab and tell my mum that I forgave everything. I had a hunger to be in that dry humming atmosphere with the green and brown jars of chemicals and the machines; it would welcome me now; I could disintegrate in its dark. I argued my case fiercely, but Árab was unmoved.

We were already close enough to the glen to see its

slopes on the horizon. I saw that there was a change, the trees and the hills were sparkling, yes, but they didn't possess depth. Each thing was like a cardboard cut-out, placed against something else, successively, going back to the furthest slope I could see. I loved the rooted feeling the glen gave me normally, the sensation of it sinking into me, not only through my eyes. But this was a sparkling cardboard place.

Spence wasn't happy that I'd drunk the whole jar, and he left us to search out more mushrooms at home. I wasn't too upset. It felt strange and unequal that I was the only one going through this experience. Árab was eager to watch my response. So far I had amused him, and startled him when I walked onto the road, but we'd not waited so long for the mushrooms just for humour and surprise.

We ended up in the forest walking towards the clearing. We stopped at a bridge and watched the water flow for a few minutes. Árab threw in a stick that reminded me of an Egyptian falcon and we followed it as it twitched downstream. The forest floor was covered in sunlight that was cut up by the trees. Once again I looked at the sky through the thin branches and felt the warmth of the sunlight coursing through my body, so that I knew I must have done this as a child.

I was smoking and kept forgetting if the cigarette was lit. We'd lit up from the same match, close in to one another to shelter from the wind (but there was no wind), looking something like El Greco's *Allegory with a Monkey*. I sat down on the stump of a tree and gazed across the river.

'Say what's going through your head now,' Árab said. It was the sort of thing Ziggy said often, but for a different reason, to see if I was thinking about her. It made me think about her now. Árab wasn't content with this answer.

'Make it a stream of consciousness,' he said – he'd learnt the phrase from me – which only made me look at the river and say nothing. Then he put his face up close – it was somehow thinner, like a lantern – and said softly: 'I hate you.'

He was experimenting with me and somewhere I registered this, but still the words went through me. I knew he liked to play at being sinister. There's a line by Lorca – 'with your cloak of ghostly captains'. That was the cloak I could imagine Árab wrapped in at those times; I actually came up with the phrase 'captain ghosts' – it suited him better. He wanted to see his own fear reflected in my eyes. It was what he loved more than anything – the mystery of that fear. Why attack him for that? I began babbling words and Árab stayed close enough to listen.

I ran out of words in the end and was left to stare at the muck and roots of an upturned tree near the river. There was something creature-like about it, as though its roots were bristles and it was curled up to sleep. It was best that it slept, I thought.

We moved on towards the part of the forest that was most dense, with Árab taking the lead. The ground was soft, almost cushioned. It reminded me of walking over the humps of graves, even to the illicit feeling it gave me. I still wasn't used to the strength of colours – yellow leapt out at me – but the need to laugh was diminishing. There was nobody here, so the sense of menace diminished too, when Árab didn't inflame it.

This was the part of the glen that we'd seen the gypsy from, and I spoke about him to Árab as we passed the exact spot.

'Do you think we'll see him again?'

'What's the fascination with gypsies?'

'Non-existent,' I said. 'I dreamt about him, though.'

He wanted to hear the dream, but the effect of relating irrational things in my irrational state was like lighting a candle in daylight. I don't know how much of the dream I told him – perhaps all of it, since I remember him being interested in the detail of the red curtain.

Soon we were walking past the last few scattered trees and into the clearing, drinking up the sunlight as we climbed the hillside to the right. The top of the hill was level with the farmhouse opposite. I wasn't as dazzled as I had been on the first night in the glen when I had seen all this by moonlight. The cardboard cut-out effect was less noticeable, or just disturbed me less, and instead of visual pyrotechnics my mind presented a dark, brooding state, the kind I'd tried to induce in myself often enough.

Árab had strayed away from me, as he had done just here many times in the past, and I was able to be alone. Here it was: I could confront this state of mind at last. I was drawn to one of the three enormous trees on the horizon of the clearing, the one we called Dragon-tree, which I loved best. I walked round it, almost as if I were tethered to it. I found the words that most nearly described what I felt: it didn't matter to me that they weren't my own. I mumbled them, smiling I'm sure – and must have looked like a madman. What did that matter? I was at the heart of the tree. Its brooding branches were my own thoughts, except that I had none, only the words: 'Red river, red river.'

Árab was approaching me, and I moved down the hill towards him. He could see in my face how happy I was – I saw that in his own eyes. We stood and looked across to the farmhouse.

14

I was feeling both lost after the mushrooms experience and on the verge of something. The light was dark for a few days. I didn't see lightning on the horizon or have any flashbacks, and I didn't chase Spence up for more mushrooms. He did a disappearing act anyway. It was close to the end of the school year and people were starting to go missing.

Lunchtime still meant heading for the centre. I made my way to the library now, to ransack the bookshelves for truth. It took me a while to start on the Religion section, and then only because the occult books were there. Just the word 'occult' brought back the memory of that day.

I made what I could of a few pages of Madame Blavatsky, which was nothing. Books were too long, language too slow. Another problem I had was the existence of other people: they appeared suddenly from around the corner of a shelf or sat down beside you with a string shopping bag. I couldn't think them away, though I whipped up a wind in my head to try to.

There was one book I looked at, about tape recordings of silence which, when they were amplified and speeded up – or slowed down, I forget – produced sounds like voices. Not any voices, but voices of the famous dead. Churchill's was one of them.

I was desperate. I took the book to the counter and waited my turn. The girl, the librarian, had black bobbed hair and an endearing way of turning books round and opening up the covers: I felt the cracking of the spines of new books inside me. I couldn't present this trash to her, I knew.

Something calming was released in me and I was able to put the book back. I looked through the music section, finding titles of songs, blues and jazz songs mostly, that released some more of the drug. *There is a Balm in Gilead* was one track. I brought the record to the girl, but she was gone.

Then I remembered the book shop in the mirrored arcade where there really was an occult shelf. I went there (I still had ten minutes), considered astrology, but put *The Dictionary of the Occult* in my pocket. I'd never stolen anything before. It didn't matter. I needed it.

I managed to see out the afternoon before rushing home with the book. I hadn't shown it to anyone – I didn't see Árab – and in my bedroom I concealed it in another book and sat back on the bed and read.

My eyes kept glancing over to the tape deck in the corner.

What if the voices-of-the-dead book wasn't so

crazy? I could tape the silence in the room. After all, Aunt Bea had died through there, through that wall. I pressed the record button and listened.

I heard the birds in the tree outside the window, the droning of the TV downstairs. Then, when I was about to stop the tape, my mum began shouting on me, not stopping to listen. I pulled the tape out of the deck, ran downstairs, past her, and put it into the music centre in the living room. She followed me in and I played the tape back. 'That's what you sound like, that's what it's like.' She pointed, hurt, to a plate of food on the table. I had my coat on after that and was outside.

I'd surprised myself. I went to the Square and phoned Árab from a phone-box. He didn't want to go out. I eventually persuaded him to meet me at the pylon. I waited there for him, though he should have reached it before me. I noticed his darkened eyes.

I wanted to speak about yesterday; in fact I exhausted myself with useless talk. I told him all about the books in the library and the occult book. He liked the phrase 'voices of the dead'.

'I wonder if a dead person's voice changes,' he said. 'In a seance, say. Does it go crackly and high-pitched?' He wasn't taking me seriously. 'Why can't you accept what happened for what it was?' he asked.

'I want to know what it was.'

'You were stoned, that's all. Stoned.'

15

Written on the back of a torn envelope on the mantelpiece was a message to phone Stephen. I was confused. I left it and went upstairs. The next morning I slept in for school. School.

I got to learn what the mysterious message was about. Stephen was somebody in school who'd been my best friend once, long before Árab. He was going on holiday in a week's time, but the friend he was to be going with had pulled out, and he was asking me now. My mum had already said yes for me.

'Where to?'

'Venice. Well, not exactly Venice – Lido de Jesolo. You can get to Venice easy from there. There's one drawback.'

'Only one?'

We would be travelling by bus and ferry and it would take three days, with a night spent in London. I felt numb. This thing had come out of the blue. Mum had agreed to it. She'd agreed because it wasn't Árab.

That last week of school died out, with just some sightings of Ziggy and a phone call to Árab. I told him about Venice and he managed two or three words on the subject. He was full of talk about assaulting the headmaster in assembly, throwing rotten food at him. The red mist was intensifying: I found it strange that the mushrooms seemed to have exacerbated things.

Since Ziggy was still being remote, I would let her hear about Venice from Árab. It didn't matter to me.

I packed my summer things, which were my winter things. The bus journey didn't put me off: it would give me time to think, to read at night under the reading light, going through Europe, with only a short space of motorway visible, the people all around me sleeping. I liked roads.

The books I brought with me were *Winter Trees* and the three other thin Sylvia Plath books. Stephen would get bored and pick one of the books up from time to time and put it back down. I advised him against one, calling it 'heavy', which he wouldn't let me forget. He'd tell me not to eat certain things because they were 'heavy'. Our luggage was 'heavy'.

The part of the journey I liked best was on the first night, when we were in England and the landscape resembled the glen. I was thinking about pylons and imagining the harlequin-like clowns of Rousseau's *Carnival Evening* in the fields. Strangely, it was the pylons that felt eerier.

I did get tired of the journey and the hot sticky feeling of my crotch in the same jeans night after night, so that I could have cried with happiness when I saw the ugly buildings of Jesolo. We were not received royally – two sixteen-year-old boys with little money. From the brown paper bag with our 'saved meal' we took a pear each and the cartons of juice and went quickly onto the street.

The street was soft and brightly coloured and the air was warm, with maybe a harvest moon in the sky (something about it seemed strange). There were bars with tables and chairs spilling onto the pavement and we wondered if we would get served in one. It would be the first time for both of us. I felt courageous, or still numb, or just tired, and went in one bar and got two beers. We drank them sitting at the tables outside: they were like the picnic tables in the glen that I'd pushed into the Calder several times. The beer was very cold and warmed us perfectly.

On the way back to the hotel, drunk after three expensive beers, we stopped at a shop that sold newspapers and things that nobody bought at night to glance up at the magazines with their explicit covers. We waited until the next night before buying one, making an arrangement whereby the person not reading the magazine walked the corridors of the hotel for twenty minutes.

Venice we saved for the third day. I had already run out of things to say to Stephen, but he was a joker, and we got by on comic observations of the harassed ticket-inspector on the bus to the boat and the drunk on the boat singing Edith Piaf. I must have been laughing very dryly because he would impersonate my laughter, especially when I hadn't in fact got the joke.

I felt let down by the sight of Venice on the horizon, until the boat swung further round and I saw its southern edge. There was a flurry of boats there, and I warmed to the chaos. My first instinct was to become lost and, not having a map yet, it was easy. Stephen recognized the streets we doubled back on, which meant that when we knew where we were, we also knew that we didn't want to be there. I was still dizzy from the boat.

I stopped in one of the squares while Stephen bought pizza from an open-front shop and I let the crowds flow round me. Underneath a statue close to an imposing church I saw what looked like an old gypsy woman haranguing a young blonde, a tourist obviously. I found myself staring at the old woman's face in much the same way Árab stared at my gran's. Just then, I didn't miss anybody. I remembered them like remembering a dream.

I arranged a time and a place to meet up if we lost each other – five, outside Harry's Bar – and waited a half-hour more before I engineered the loss.

Stephen had stopped to eat again, ice-cream this time, and I turned sharply down one street, and another and another, until I came to a deserted spot. It was beautiful, the sudden shift into a desolate landscape.

There was a place that I wanted to find. I had written down the address and carried it in my back pocket, and with the map I had just bought I caught the vaporetto to Dorsoduro. Even from the stop it was quite far and not easy to find. The place was San Nicolo dei Mendicoli. I couldn't believe that this was it. It was a church that was used in the film *Don't Look Now*. I had an image in my mind of a vast white edifice and gargoyles: this was red brick.

Inside was no better. I thought that perhaps over there, in that recess, there had been a railing that the blind woman had run her hand across, but it must have been sleight-of-hand that made the ceiling seem so high up when John Baxter had fallen. I looked for the English words that told me the history of the place, and there was no mention of the film. It didn't surprise me. Walking up and down and across the church was a stumpy priest who didn't acknowledge my 'Hello'; I saw that he had rosary beads in his hands. The church was open for tourists twice a day, but only briefly, and grudging consent was written into the little man's brow. Still, he was impressive in his contemplation.

I took the wrong vaporetto and watched horrified as Venice turned away from me. I tried to see the time on people's wrists: I was unconfident about asking, or speaking at all. If I wasn't gone for hours I'd still make it for five.

I stepped off the vaporetto at the first landing stage. It was my intention to head back, not to stay and explore the place and make myself late, but I was struck by the emptiness, an absence of people that I'd had to search for in Venice. I started to walk to see what was beyond the wall.

I didn't know that San Michele, where I was, was Venice's cemetery. There was one man strolling a graveyard away, a newspaper folded under his arm, and then, five minutes later, there was an old Italian couple. The strolling man was a tourist but the couple had brought flowers. I'd never seen anything like this, the bodies stacked five high, each in its coffin-size recess, with the names and dates and photographs of the dead. There were flowers too, mostly artificial, but some not, and it was their smell, I imagined, that perfumed the air. But it was a cloying, sickly sweetness, and I wondered if this was the smell of death. An island given over to death.

The man, a well-dressed gent, strolled towards me. He was carrying the *Daily Telegraph*. I thought of that later, because when he asked me if I knew the way to Diaghilev's tomb I spoke to him as though to a foreigner. It was just that he pronounced Diaghilev correctly, I suppose.

I made the rendezvous with Stephen and was astonished to find him with two girls. They were sisters, one clearly much younger than the other, as young as twelve or thirteen. I heard the young girl say, 'Which one do you want?', and noticed how slurred her words were. She had been drinking. All three had been drinking: Stephen displayed guiltily the miniature liqueur bottles in his bag.

'We might get somewhere with the older sister, we can fight over her,' he said.

'No, leave it,' I told him, but not with weariness – more like authority. We were walking away from them, ignoring their taunts.

The rest of the holiday unwound itself, disclosing nothing that was new to me, except perhaps how much I depended for life on Árab and Ziggy. I had thought that, after experiencing the illumination down the glen, I could have dispensed with them easily. Ziggy and Árab equalled life, but my illumination equalled more life. Comforting to put it mathematically.

16

I didn't enjoy the journey home, and by the time we reached England I was in no mood to people forests with harlequins or pore over the slender, violent poems again, though I found talking easier and I was a good friend to Stephen for a day. A down side was that the red wine I was bringing back for Árab's parents spilled out on the bus and muddied the floor.

Ziggy had been phoning when I was away and leaving messages. She mustn't have known I was abroad and my family didn't enlighten her, which angered me. I was back and angry within seconds.

I wanted to walk out to see her, but after staring down at my opened suitcase I saw that I had nothing to put on. I pushed back the hangers in the wardrobe to reveal one stonewashed flowery shirt, my least favourite: but it would do. Ziggy, if she was missing me, would forgive it.

I needed time, but I knew that I had to draw the strands of my life together. It was always blowing hot and cold too easily with Árab and Ziggy, and I could be at fault. I sulked too much. I posed too much, wanting to stand in the shadows of doorways like a lean outsider, breaking down when I was ruffled a little, by Ziggy's unblinking stare for one thing, which she had perfected. We were ready to sleep together now. I'd been avoiding talking about it because I wanted an instinct of bodies to decide for us in the dark, without words, but it wasn't going to happen like that.

I met her turning the corner near her house after Marie had answered the door and not invited me in. Marie's boyfriend Simon had been there with his hand on the hallway wall. He was grinning inanely and I saw more clearly what Árab disliked in him.

'You're back,' Ziggy said.

She let the dog up into her room for once, and it was bounding about on the bed, licking her face. I said I was back from Venice.

'I know, I've just seen Árab,' she said.

'You have?'

'Yes,' she said.

'... How is he?'

'Angry about something, someone, I don't know,' she said.

'I know. I've been having that problem with him. He wanted to assault White before the end ...' I had got to the word 'end' when she stopped me.

'I've been seeing someone else,' she said.

She might as well have banged my face off a concrete slab.

'I thought you should know.' She meant it to sound lame, but it was defiant.

'And I am supposed to say ... what?' I looked at her pale freckled skin, the outline of the bones in her face, and I wanted to mash it all. Her hair was grown. Was it really such a long time since I'd seen her? How long had she been seeing this someone?

'How long?' I asked.

'It doesn't matter.'

'No, it matters.'

'I don't know, a month, but it didn't start a month ago, it's only started now,' she said.

I felt a shock go through me. 'Is it Árab?' I asked her.

'Árab? *Árab?* ... No.' She clutched at the change in atmosphere, amused now. 'What made you think it was Árab?'

I let myself go then, and shouted into her face as I held her jaw. That coy way she'd asked 'What made you think ... ?' honestly looking for me to list the signs she'd given.

Ziggy's father almost fell into the room, shouting at me to get out. I'd released Ziggy's face from my grip before he came in, otherwise I'm certain he would have hit me. His appearance on the scene did stun me, and I was mechanically picking up what I needed in order to leave. When I reconstructed it all in my head later I observed that Ziggy wasn't crying even at that point. She had never seen me cry, never would, but I cried there in the hallway looking back over my shoulder.

I walked the streets until it was late, until I began to feel some pride in having walked so far: it helped displace some of the jealous rage I felt. This hadn't happened to me before, rejection like this, yet it was familiar. A clothes-dummy in a shop window stared at me in a yellow light. There was no life in anything. Not just because of what had happened. The landscape was a sick vacancy. The world was death and sick vacancy. Sometimes you noticed it. That's all.

I thought of the gypsywoman haranguing the blonde in Venice, and I said to her in my head 'Don't stop. Harangue her some more.' Another picture: Ziggy's dog licking her face. It was *his* tongue licking it. She was loving it all, lapping it up, his licking, her loving it. I cried in the hallway. Didn't that count?

I was about as far from Árab's as it was possible to be and still be in the town, when it occurred to me that he might know something. Hadn't Ziggy been round to see him? It was late, though. Not so late that nobody would be up, but too late to call round. No – there were no rules. The world can't be dead and still have rules. That wasn't true. I would think it out later; now I had to reach Árab.

My mind should probably have shut down through depression, but it didn't, and as I went diagonally across town I imagined a map of the streets I walked along and filled it out with the other places I knew. I'd never imagined the place as a whole before. It was kite-shaped, if you pictured the bottom tip of the kite on the left and the sides curving up to the right, something like a 'y'. Árab's house, then mine, then Ziggy's, could be plotted on the cup shape of the y, from left to right. It formed a lopsided grin.

Árab's bedroom light was on and I thought that there was nothing else for it but to throw muck at the window. He must have heard me rooting about outside, or else he just happened to look out: the window opened and he was telling me to wait there. Something in me still wanted to hit the window, and the thought of that amused me and relaxed me. I think Árab thought I was happy as he let me inside.

'I can see you searching my face,' I said to him in the room, 'so I know that you know.'

'That's a strange way to talk,' he said.

'Ziggy was round tonight. She told you what's been going on.'

'Yes,' he said, as if conceding defeat. There was some sympathy in that 'yes'.

'So what has been going on?' I asked. He seemed about to shrug. 'Just tell me what you know.'

'How much do you know?'

'Nothing except that she's seeing somebody.'

He was a musician, played bass in a band she'd seen. It started when she was sick. She was still going out at night, but not with me. He was older than her by four years, wore leather, and Árab had spoken to him and he was all right. She hadn't brought him to Árab's house, but she arranged a meeting before I left for Venice. She'd called just after I called. It worried him that that looked bad, but he'd not done anything wrong. As a matter of fact he'd turned down the offer to join the band. He thought that I had nothing to fear – this guy wouldn't hang around for long.

'What can I say? I don't want the two of you to split up any more than you do. No you don't. You only feel like that now. You have been sort of neglecting her.'

I didn't understand him.

'It's been noticeable,' he said. 'I'm not accusing you. I thought for a while ... this isn't easy to say ... I thought she might be coming on to me a little, but it was because you were being such a bastard. I knew that. If you want me to nit-pick and point out every single thing you've done ...'

I wanted him to.

He wouldn't.

We shut up and went to sleep.

17

When I was three or four I had a toy gramophone – I have to use that word, it was so old-fashioned looking – that was bright red and yellow, with a large horn and a huge round-headed arm. I had to turn a handle to make the music come out, nursery rhymes sung to tinkling music. I loved it and it kept me amused until, two or three years later, I was able to use the long wooden record player downstairs, playing the singles that had gathered dust since – well, before I can remember.

That is what the beginning of my second experience with mushrooms reminds me of. There were six of us, we could have emerged out of that bright horn, a harlequinade with Árab and myself jostling to be leader. I watched Árab's face grow yellow under a streetlight, as we laughed at nothing over and over. We moved into the shadows of the glen and walked with heads thrust unnaturally back, looking at the purple sky – purple to my eyes, at least – and the stars hypnotically pulsing. Somebody, Ryan I think, was singing 'See-saw, Margery Daw' madly and badly. My laughter sounded strange to me – tinny. I probably walked like a three-year-old too, my knees lifted high as I judged (misjudged) the undulations of the earth.

It was the night of the day following the night spent at Árab's. I'd begun the morning with a phone call home to say I was alive. I was lucky – mum had gone to my aunt's in Paisley for the weekend and Stephen had put my pillows down inside the bed for gran's headcount. Stephen's voice was heavy with innuendo. Afterwards I realized that he thought I'd spent the night with Ziggy. It was what might have happened.

Árab simply wasn't going to talk about the ugliness between Ziggy and me, and it seemed that that was final. I felt it surround me all day, like the unwashed shirt I hated so much. There wasn't the usual intensity between us; in fact he seemed determined to spread himself thinly. We crossed the road to a house opposite where a friend of his lived (he was more family than friend). Phone calls were made and a circle was formed round the kitchen table. Ryan and Brobyn were there. I wasn't comfortable, but I would show Árab that I could hold my own.

It wasn't long before we were talking about mushrooms. One of the two that I didn't know spoke and said that it would be easy to find some. Árab was reluctant to believe him, as I was, but he swore on his mother's grave.

We found them growing in a place we'd walked across countless times, the first hill as you step out into the clearing: usually we walked over this and the small stream to the hill that had Dragon-tree at its top. We brought them, hundreds of them, back to the kitchen and made tea from them, which we let cool and put into any bottles and jars that were about.

We drank this at night, just as it was getting dull and the streetlights came on. There was no way of knowing the strength of what we took. My state of mind after Ziggy's revelation worried me, but I masked my fear with the bravado that comes from male company. Árab's face turned yellow; we were laughing at nothing ...

Once the trip started, it was like being dropped into a sewer and the lid replaced. You were confined in a state of mind. I had been trying not to think about Ziggy; now it was impossible to think about her, beyond wanting her to be here. The hilarity was drying up and enthusing about the psychedelic landscape paled: time was cut up into brief frames. I didn't like these strangers being with us. One of them, the one who found the mushrooms, had teeth like a shark's. I was insisting through the confusion on staying, but Árab wanted to leave the glen, because being in the street would be harder. Árab won out and we traipsed back through the forest. Somebody pointed to a school nearby, not our school, and we went up to it. I wanted not to go in there, but once we found an open door inevitably we went inside. It was one long corridor that seemed to lead nowhere, its walls covered in graffiti-art. This was too much, the bright reds and yellows.

I leant into an alcove and slid down the wall. Everyone else was either still or pacing the same few yards. It seemed we were in a kind of contemplation phase. Bizarre ideas were being exchanged – not exactly exchanged, uttered. I focused on Ryan who was mumbling repeatedly 'blinding light'. Árab looked to be still in control of himself. The idea of flight gripped me, but I knew that in this narrow space flying would be difficult.

A man appeared in the corridor and asked if we were the last of the night school lot, which solved the mystery of why the door had been open. It must have dawned on him that we were not a part of anything that should have been there. His voice became thundery and swept us outside.

I attempted again to steer us towards the glen, but it was no use, we were into the maze of streets with their white houses and humped-up little lawns. I knew this area, I had walked through it with Árab, but I didn't know it well – it wasn't a sacred place. Walking didn't feel like it was over cotton wool but along a railway line. The blurred lamplight from several of the houses nauseated me.

I was singing the nursery rhyme now, hoping that Ryan would pick it up again. I probably sang very quietly. We got to the bridge over the High Common Road.

Brobyn had fallen over in the middle of the bridge and wouldn't get up. Árab was dominating the space around him, listening closely to whatever Brobyn muttered – his name and address, as I learnt later, which he kept repeating. Árab, when I spoke to him the next day on the phone, made much of this, saying that it was what an epileptic would do. Árab had a horror of epilepsy.

It took me a long time to be able to concentrate on what was happening on the bridge, but eventually I helped lift Brobyn up. The good thing that came out of it was that the two strangers had gone on and we didn't see them again. The glen was now far enough away that the thought of escape into it wasn't a comfort any more.

The drizzle brought comfort though, the feel of the rain and the fungal smell it brought out of the grass verges. The worst effects of the mushrooms wore off slightly. I led the way for a spell and took us down a road that I knew wound out of town. A few hundred yards along it there was a derelict building, a very old building that was still intact. We went inside to stare at the huge rusted wheel that was propped against a stone slab.

I was smoking happily and beginning to talk again, though the other three were not nearly themselves yet. Ryan was being more coherent about the blinding light, out of which he'd expected his dead father to step. He made a promise to himself not to touch mushrooms again, which even then, coming out of the throes of a bad experience myself, I was cynical about. I had my smoking hand leaning on a spoke of the giant wheel, and, close up, I studied the wheel and thought about it. It was straight out of one of my poems. I loved the thought of encountering every image I had used, sitting and smoking next to them. What else would be there? Knives, scorpions, bridges, foxgloves, fire.

Brobyn wanted to go home and wanted a taxi to take him home. His eyes were bloodshot and he was restless to the point of being nasty, but in a way that none of the rest of us took seriously. The spectacle of him bobbing about like a frenzied glove puppet only made us laugh harder, until he started to hit his head against a wall.

I helped Árab to hold him, putting my hand on his cut forehead and my knee into the back of his leg and easing him backwards. He managed to hit the wall twice more, which meant that my hand was cut badly. I said to him as a joke, 'We're blood brothers now.'

Brobyn wouldn't go anywhere with Árab or me, but he didn't object to Ryan, and we didn't object to letting Ryan walk him home. It turned out that Ryan abandoned him just a short distance from where we were, which led to some trouble when Brobyn was picked up and driven home by a family friend. Ryan didn't come back. I was already anticipating the sorrow I was going to feel over Ziggy, but I wasn't stopping to lend it a hand. My blood-smeared hand. I was in a delirious state almost indistinguishable from joy. When Árab said 'You all right?' I knew that it didn't look like joy.

18

It was the emptiest summer I could remember. It was also one of the stormiest – literally – through August. I stayed in my room. I might as well have counted the leaves on the tree outside the window.

It wouldn't be true to say that I didn't sleep. My dreams grew strange even for dreams because I overslept. They were too many to count, but they danced around the central dream of the knifeman and the dying cattle and running upstairs, which kept recurring: it always ended at the same moment. People worried about me – my family, not Árab though, or he didn't show it – but I sneered at them until their own defences took over and anger replaced concern. It was what I wanted.

Árab came round sometimes but I went to him and the glen less often. The glen became so sacred that I had to purify myself before I could go there. Everything had to be right. If I took a book with me it had to be the right one, but perhaps taking a book at all was a wrong idea. So it went on, and the truth was that I was growing afraid of the place.

I didn't even have photographs to console me. I used to be critical of Árab for bringing a camera with him to the glen, so I couldn't ask him for photographs now. I was growing nostalgic for something that had only just gone, or could even be still there. I hated feeling this. It was one of my sayings, 'Don't look back.' My mistake had been to look over my shoulder in Ziggy's.

I looked up Ziggy's phone number, as though I'd forgotten it, the night before school started again. I actually had forgotten my code for remembering it, until, seeing the number next to her dad's name in the phone book, it suddenly came back to me. 'You owe one sex, fine!' Irony. I put the phone down for a minute.

Marie answered when I did call. When she came back on, and asked me how I was, my voice trembled. I sensed her pitying me in my predicament, and so ended the call. She would tell Ziggy I'd phoned, she said. *You already have*, I thought.

I spent my first lunch hour with Árab looking for more mushrooms; half-heartedly, since we didn't have enough time to get to the glen. I felt it was a case of clinging to what we'd lost – that wildness. In the afternoon I discovered that I'd lost my Indian maiden too. Now we had a man to talk about Wilfred Owen.

I found out more, through another girl, about the bass player, but not what I wanted to know: if he was sleeping with her. In English I sat nearer the back and was able to look. There was nothing I could be sure about. I'd expect her to be louder, more buoyant, but she was the opposite of that, without being timid. Older, I suppose. There was no ribbon.

It was at exactly three o'clock that the beginning of the end occurred, Árab finally satisfying his madness, with a bag of putrid tomatoes slung through the air. I can see now that something was ending from that moment. There were no consequences just then, since Árab had made sure he blended in with the crowd, but there would be. I knew it. He'd said too much. Even I didn't hear about it from him.

We met at the gate, where I'd been waiting for him. I saw again that girl who blew smoke with her kisses. She noticed me. Árab strolled into view with the most composed, heroic expression I'd seen his face adopt, which is saying something, but I still disapproved. It was a needless act.

He told me the whole story. Then, as an afterthought, he said: 'Ziggy wants you back.'

'What?'

'It looks like it. She's finished with that guy, not the other way round, and she's sorry, apparently.'

19

Ziggy arranged a meeting through Árab and the place she chose was the holy hill (our name for it), the hill that sloped up to the field with the Dalí crutches. I told him we needed to be by ourselves. Of course, he said – but sometimes with Árab you had to insist on the obvious.

I was there first, walking in a thin mist. 'The mist-breathing clarity' was a phrase I thought up. I wanted to feel wide-open. I knew that there was a freshness in my face.

Ziggy walked out from the edge of the forest, wearing red, a colour she said she would never wear – even from a distance I could see that it was her sister's dress. She had a long black shawl too, and something, a black shoulder bag it looked like, which she stared into. She still hadn't seen me. I was lying back in the long grass of the hill.

I waved to her. I was a long way off, but she would see me if she looked round. I got up and careered downhill, being noticed finally by a flustered Ziggy. She stuffed something yellow into the bag.

The features of her face came into focus like a painting. I could make out her expression now. It was a cross between wistful and sorrowful. I wanted to appeal to her wistfulness, but it was the sorrow that touched me more. Not that anything like that passed through my mind.

I said a muffled hello – muffled by the collar of my coat, which was turned up and buttoned over my mouth. She put her hand over her mouth and said hello back. It was funny enough to break the ice. Being with her felt natural and right, and I thought 'No, don't explain', but she seemed to think that she must. We were walking side by side and she took some yellow sheets of paper from her bag. 'It's all there,' she said, 'I want you to read it now. I'll walk on.' That was what happened. I walked slowly and read while she made her way to the swing park and waited.

I picked up that I had bled her dry emotionally, with my 'smaller-than-average heart'. But the good thing was that she wrote 'Baby' – in a jokey way, perhaps, but still affectionate. Meant.

I put the letter, folded along its creases, into my coat pocket, and walked towards the swings. There seemed to be no wind at all except in the branches of the trees. They were so beautiful, the leaves still on these ones, the lightest colour of green imaginable.

This was a good place to stand and look over to where Ziggy was sitting on a swing and to the hill behind. I walked out from that sheltered place and went down to stand a few feet from her. Without saying so, she wanted to know what I thought about the letter. There was a coyness in her, very different from the coyness that had enraged me before, when she had asked why I thought she was seeing Árab. Every time I looked at her she seemed to be in profile, with her head looking to the side and down or else lifted suddenly like a wolf howling at the moon; though not like a wolf, in fact, but displaying a vulnerability in the exposed veins of her neck.

'It's astonishing,' I said, 'I didn't know that you could write like that.'

'You think so?' she said, suddenly pleased. 'But what about what I'm saying?'

'Hard on me.'

'I didn't think so.'

Soon I was gathering sticks for a fire. Ziggy said nothing. I felt that she was secretly pleased, content to let me roam around in a different state of mind from hers. That almost never happened when we were together in her room, I thought. Every word or movement would be watched for what might come out, and we would goad one another to know exactly what was meant. I felt obscurely that this might be a new beginning. I tried to be expert at building the fire.

Ziggy had a shoelace necklace on, which I'd seen without noticing (how could I not have noticed it?) and, once the fire was started, she took it off and said: 'Burn this.' It was difficult for her, standing on the swing and having to use both hands to untie it, and she ended up with one of the chains coiled round her. The command to burn the necklace was melodramatic and it hurt me, knowing what it meant, though it was supposed to please me. That this was his present to her.

It was a good fire, fragrant somehow, and I stood in the way of the smoke so that it would get into my hair and clothes. I appreciated its heat on my face.

'How are my lips?' Ziggy asked, squatting down next to me. 'They feel cracked.' She was running her tongue over them. I sang a line about cracked country lips.

'Don't,' she said, turning away from me. 'I was asking you seriously.'

'They're not cracked,' I said, 'just dry. Maybe you shouldn't sit with your face to the fire.'

She turned back round and kissed me. We kissed for a few minutes and then she settled her head in my lap. She was curled up as if she was cold, but I brushed her cheek with my hand and it felt hot. I stroked her hair and she said, 'Keep doing that.'

After a while she asked me about the letter again. I found it difficult to speak 'about us', as she wanted.

'I'll write a letter for you,' I said. 'When I get back tonight.'

'But I'm here now,' she said, half getting up and leaning on an elbow. She wasn't leaning back. There was nothing languorous about her now, only insistent.

A horse appeared, from out of nowhere it seemed, which was when I realized how dark it had become. I'd seen joggers here at night, but not this, a horse with a woman rider. The woman shouted out as she passed us: 'You mustn't light fires here.'

Ziggy had a thought. 'We could be seen. Do you think Árab's out there?' But she wasn't inhibited by the thought and climbed over me laughing. Then she stood up close to me, with her back to the fire.

'It's a gypsy dance,' she said, clicking her fingers. 'I saw a film last night. They were real gypsies in it.' It was so typically how I imagined a gypsy dance to look that I didn't believe her.

'Sing something,' she said.

I knew one verse of a gypsy song. It wasn't difficult to improvise a tune, sung with my best Romany intonation –

The crack of doom
Is coming soon.
Let it come.
It doesn't matter.

'I thought gypsies were optimistic,' she said, stopping for a second as if I'd stunned her. 'Typical of you,' she said, and started to dance again. 'Anything depressing or boring or slow-moving, that's you, you're right in there.'

20

'You were seen.'

Whoever she was, she whispered the confidence to us conspiratorially, as if that bare statement could be of any help. I had been summoned, just as I had been before, but more ceremonially this time, not with a scrawl on the back of a registration slip; Ziggy as well, to the headmaster's office. I felt like a small child again, needing to go to the toilet but afraid to move. Ziggy was being the epitome of cool, but I knew her better. She was sweating too.

It was torture to have to stand awkwardly beside her after we had been so memorably at ease. I stood with my hands like lead weights dangling from my wrists, trying to stifle the gypsy verse that was replaying in my head. It had been sensual and direct last night: not now. Was this the doom it mentioned?

The headmaster's door opened and the headmaster and a man I recognized appeared. They shook hands – not for the first time, I felt sure. They were probably inside there shaking hands five or six times and agreeing about everything (it's how it appeared). I remembered now that it was Brobyn's dad. White looked at us and blanked us out.

Next was the deputy's appearance. I was intrigued by his approach: he looked as though he planned to be very gentle and solicitous and then thought better of it. He was just standing there, yards from me, staring. Ziggy laughed. I realized that he was imitating me, adopting my slouched posture, hands in pockets. He smiled when I straightened up and shook his head slowly. What was he about to say? 'Maverick'? He walked into White's room, knocking but not waiting.

I hadn't seen Brobyn since the night he collapsed on the bridge. Jesus, I thought, is that it? Maybe he's been sick ever since. It didn't explain why Ziggy would be in trouble, or why Árab and Ryan wouldn't be. That was as far as logic would take me. Instead of being able to think, I had a picture in my mind of my brother Michael and me in the long rough beach grass of Lytham, St Anne's, sitting either side of our mum who is wearing dark glasses: I am wearing a hat with 'maverick' written on it.

The deputy reappeared with a smiling frown. He asked Ziggy if she had seen the nurse yet. She immediately grew pale. He took her off with him, having thought about placing a comforting hand on her shoulder, if his awkwardly extended arm meant that.

Which left me alone with the Mary-statue, panicking.

Five, ten minutes passed, and then it really was my turn. White called me inside. I wanted to tell him, as I looked round his room, that I had been here before, aged five, but he had only one expression, deadly serious, and it was directed at me now.

Mr Brobyn had lodged a complaint some weeks ago (he said) that his son had been brought home ill after spending an evening in the company of three pupils of the school and two others. They were trying to trace these two but they were aware of the identities of the three pupils: I was one of them. He was making no accusations but he suspected the involvement of drugs. What did I have to say?

'Which evening?' I asked, making it clear from the outset that I would tell him nothing. There was more interrogation and more frustration, and he let slip Árab's name. Eventually everything seemed to turn on this one issue, of Árab's involvement. Did he supply us with drugs? was the final exasperated inquiry.

'No,' I said.

There was a silence and then a table-thump and finally an obscure threat. He told me that any pupils having a sexual relationship would face expulsion.

I didn't have a sexual relationship with Árab, I found myself thinking for one confused moment, until I thought about Ziggy being taken to see the nurse. Surely they couldn't do that, examine her? 'This is just the beginning,' were the words I was left with on release.

Árab had to be warned – panic was beating in me once again, after the disturbing calm I had just experienced – and Ziggy found. Árab was easily found, since the lunch-bell was ringing and we'd already arranged to meet. When I got to the school gate Ziggy was with him.

I can remember that moment, when the three of us looked at each other.

Árab spoke first. 'They know I threw the tomatoes at White and they know I was unconscious at the party, they *think* I've been bringing gear into this place, and ... Do you know this?'

'Some of it,' I said, fascinated.

'They think that either him or you made me pregnant,' Ziggy said. 'I'm not pregnant,' she said quickly. 'That woman on the horse last night – it must have been her ... But I don't know her.'

'Must have been her what?'

'Somebody saw us last night and seems to think we had sex and definitely identified me, and they're guessing it was one of you two. There's been a rumour going around that I'm pregnant anyway.'

'I've not heard it ... What's happening?' I looked at Árab. 'If they know about you attacking White, why do they need anything else?'

Árab's voice deepened, as it did when he was in a situation that might embarrass him, though none ever really did. That deep laughing voice saved him somehow.

'They want to have a cast-iron case for expelling me, or they're thinking about bringing the police in. Fuck knows how long they've been working on it.'

'Something White said made me think the nurse was examining you, to check you were still a virgin,' I said to Ziggy.

'No, idiot ... What did he say?'

21

There was a dwarf-figure, small and raging and red, inside a suitcase. I said 'I can handle this,' but to soothe him I had to become a kind of minstrel-harlequin. I woke up remembering the lines I had been singing –

> I saw yellow, then I saw red
> I said the first words that came into my head

It was the last dream I had in my bed for a week – the last night I spent there for a week.

The summons to the headmaster turned out not to be the crack of doom. The nurse had spoken to Ziggy about pregnancy, with advice about how to avoid it. Ziggy added that she had been motherly. When Ziggy heard what had been said to me, about expulsion, she was furious and wanted to hit someone: not just anyone, but the girl who had been the source of the rumours. (It made me stop to think when I heard who it was: I always thought she seemed extraordinarily dead.)

They appeared to know that I hadn't been with Árab when he threw the tomatoes. The nurse's report back must have cleared Ziggy. The questions about drugs were asked with less and less conviction. It was the deputy head that I talked some of this through with, though my talk was monosyllabic. He was concerned for my spiritual welfare again, also about my relations with the world. He exploded when I said 'The world is run by the dead,' and nothing he tried could make him appear unruffled again.

'Tomorrow I'll know,' Árab said as we met up once more, this time at the end of the day. Ziggy, who was always somewhere else by then, had come to be with us. 'I've been given twenty-four hours' grace,' he told us with a grin. He drew the index finger of his right hand across his neck and made a whistling sound, saying, 'Then it's ...'

'You don't know that,' I said. He switched from

amusement to anger, with Ziggy backing him up.

'You think there won't be consequences?' she said.

I snapped out of my dreamlike conformity and saw the situation we were in. With the two of them standing there looking angrily at me, I knew I didn't want solitude. This was a chance to realize what I had waited for, what I had come not to expect: the three of us as one. Deep down I had been prepared to sacrifice Árab before.

'We could go somewhere,' Ziggy said. It was as if she had uttered a magic formula. Nobody said anything at first.

'There's an empty farmhouse in the glen,' Árab said.

'That's a working farm,' I said.

'You don't know what I'm talking about,' he said.

'What are you talking about?' Ziggy asked him.

'I'm talking about a place you don't know. You', he said, looking at me, 'turned back before we could reach it. Remember where Ryan thought he saw a stag? Another two miles across the moors.'

Across the moors: it would be a good isolated place to stay, but not to get to, and I muttered some complaint such as this to Árab.

'That's true, but there's a road that goes past it, I don't know – half a mile, less.' We all brightened up and I know that I was shivering. 'If we walked out that way it would take hours, or we get wet and muddy going the glen way.'

'I vote for the road,' Ziggy said. 'But either we get wheels or you carry me.'

She wasn't serious, but it wasn't funny either.

'If I can get a car, will you drive?' Árab asked her.

'Yes,' she said.

'Tell me I'm dreaming,' I said.

'I've got my Provisional,' she said. I hadn't known that. I think she heard the little-girl boastfulness in her voice, because she asked Árab in a different voice: 'How will you get a car?'

'Spence's brother, but he'll have to kind of steal it.'

'This is going to happen,' I said, my voice heavy with irony.

Plans were made over the phone at night, but I still didn't quite believe in it. Ziggy's words about getting wheels must have stuck in my head because before the dream about the dwarf I dreamt that the three of us were clambering over a giant wheel, like a Big Dipper but still a car-wheel, that had some of its spokes missing. It broke loose from its moorings and we were falling into the sea. I didn't know if this was lucky, if the wheel would float and save us or take us under. I had about ten other dreams and then the dwarf dream.

I had problems deceiving my mum about going to school, and she had that sixth sense that I feared (in her), and was hanging back. Eventually she had to go, telling gran in my hearing to make sure I left. Gran observed me, content to be able to tell her daughter later that I had deceived her. I was wearing four layers of clothes, as we had agreed.

Ziggy arrived at my house. She was being mysterious, encouraged by my sly willingness to be kept uninformed. We had to hurry. I pointed out that she was carrying a bag. Because she was a girl, she said, it was allowed.

'I know this place,' I told her, as we cut through high flats to reach the road that would take us to the Kingsway. The flats were like the ones I imagined as Chinese shacks sometimes, or else as being made entirely of glass. 'My gran lived here with her sister before they moved in with us.' I hadn't been told yet that her musician lived there, so I couldn't see how Ziggy knew about a short cut.

There was no place to stop on the Kingsway: Árab, if he had a car, wasn't waiting there. Ziggy convinced me that she didn't know if he had got one. She was taking me to a prearranged place, then we would see. Eventually I decided to stop acting like a baby and asked her directly, 'Where are we going?' Unfortunately it came out sounding childlike.

'Here,' she said, as she took the path veering off to the left. It was an entrance to the small wood that I passed through on my way to school.

'He said to meet us by the swing,' she said. It was unpromising-looking, as we could see the tree-swing ahead with no sign of Árab. When we came up to it I held onto the wooden plank on its scruffy blue ropes, as if that could conjure him. It worked, though I didn't know it at first: the small white van that trundled over the slope-horizon contained him.

Ziggy kissed him through the open window with uninhibited joy, but that was all right, I was glad to see him too, and amazed. He was in the passenger seat, a man I didn't know beside him. It was Spence's brother. He got out of the van, understandably awkward because of his long legs, and dangled the car key below Ziggy's nose, saying just five words before he walked away: 'Take care ... of the van.'

With my back to the spare tyre and feet wedged against a wooden slat, I was prepared for the weird journey ahead. We were lucky that the roads were quiet.

Ziggy, feeling my tension, said: 'Don't worry, there's a St Christopher here.'

We arrived at the place intact: that is to say, at the spot on the road parallel to it. There was some discussion about whether we should drive off the road and risk the van on the soft earth or not. Árab didn't want tyre tracks leading obviously to the house. In the end we drove into a small scattering of beech trees where the ground was firm – I was sent to check it first. When we left the van there and trusted to Árab's sense of direction we found that the ground didn't deteriorate at all, and we could have driven closer, but we needed the trees' protection to hide the van. I didn't recognize the intense feeling that flooded me. It might have been freedom and doom combined.

The farmhouse was abandoned, there was no doubting that. I opened each door expecting to see a carpet of mice unravel before me. There was no sign of any life, unless you counted the mould; not even empty beer cans. In one room, at the centre of the house, there was a fragrant smell, and I imagined a censer having been swung here.

Ziggy said: 'It's the damp you smell,' but I didn't believe her. 'Careful,' I said as she walked over carpet and stained hardboard, 'there could be a hole under that.' Every room had floorboards missing; they seemed to have been ripped out and then piled in a corner.

Upstairs was out of reach, with empty air after the second step. Árab will engineer something to get us up, I thought. Once I had been in each downstairs room I walked outside and looked at the house again. It was old, but there was a modern extension.

'This was the toilet,' Árab shouted out. He was just an arm's length away from me, on the other side of the broken frame. I looked in and saw an unplumbed toilet bowl with black leaves inside. After I turned away I heard a trickling sound and realized he was pissing. 'This is the toilet,' I heard him say to himself.

22

We survived the cold that night, just, under our coats and a dirty blanket from the van. Árab decided that we would risk being seen, and whatever other risk there was, by lighting a fire inside the house. We built it just as we would a fire in the glen, except that we made a base from stones so that the floor wouldn't catch. There was some quite dry wood, especially near the collapsed stair, and more where the van was. I woke up just once in the night, disorientated and trying to fix in my mind which house this was. It was raining outside. When I was awake enough to think, it surprised me that there was only one dripping sound inside the room where the rain got in. Ziggy was breathing heavily, but Árab was silent. So I thought, until I looked round for him and he wasn't there. It was too cold to bother about it. I went back to sleep and had one of my paralysis dreams, when I think I wake up and move about the room, then realize I'm sleeping and try to move but I'm paralysed: it feels like an electric current passes through me. I wasn't frightened by the dream: knowing Ziggy was next to me took the fear out of it.

She woke me in the morning affectionately, whispering to me that Árab was gone. When I said that he was gone in the night too, she sat up quickly.

'He's gone back, hasn't he?'

'I don't think so,' I said.

'Where else would he be?'

'The van?'

I stabbed open a tin of pears with the green-handled knife I'd brought, while Ziggy dressed and went over to the beech trees. She came back upset and angry, sure he had left us.

'We're not going back,' she said. I didn't want to anyway, and I handed her the knife and the remnants of the tin.

'We're stinking, aren't we?' she said when she was calmer.

'You tell me, you kissed my armpit this morning.'

'Error.'

'We could wash in a river.'

She wanted to leave him a note, but since he'd not left us one she changed her mind. We walked about a mile to the river; I wanted it to be further away, now that I felt cold air in my body and Ziggy's gloved hand touching me. If only this path wound its way for ribbon-miles.

The water in the river was cold but not muddy. It was as clear as a mirror, Ziggy said. We watched our own nakedness for a few moments: I was glad that we didn't splash childishly. In the cold air we dried off and put our clothes back on.

'I feel alive again,' Ziggy said.

We were close to some trees. Whatever trees they were, there was plenty of air and light being let through their leaves. They were like cages above our heads, with the bars placed far apart – very high above our heads. Though there was plenty of wood in the farmhouse – 'diseased', Ziggy called it – we looked about for wood for the fire, going back with greenish branches in our arms: I looked forward to seeing them spit. We had already lit the fire when Árab walked in, his arms also full, with food and two bottles of wine. The food was fairly scrappy. He didn't say where he'd been, but he hadn't been away all night.

'You missed this?' He was holding up a crescent-shape of wood with wooden bars sticking out of it. It must have come from a child's bed or a cot. 'I was upstairs last night.'

He had improvised a hoist to function instead of the stairs. The only surprise was that he'd done it so silently and in the dark.

'That's all the wood there is there,' he said.

We ate first, leaving the wine for night-time, and afterwards went up. The hoist was a bit too makeshift for comfort. The floor was more precarious here, with fewer floorboards. Ziggy desperately wanted to see the room that was open to the outside. It did feel strange opening the door that was still sound on its hinges, and seeing the sky and the place where we had washed and got the wood, but we couldn't go much further than the doorway. I asked Árab how he could have seen his way around last night.

'I had the lighter,' he said 'and the moon out here. Orion was right there, above that telegraph pole, if that's what it is.'

'But it was raining last night,' I said.

'I know, I didn't sleep here.'

'Where then?' Ziggy said.

'Through there.'

He led us along the landing into a doorless room and held open the curtain to let us see. The floor was intact and one of Árab's coats was there. An old fireplace was the room's one feature. Something cracked and I saw Ziggy stooping down. She picked up a shard of mirror that was like a blade, looked at me in it and smiled. It made me think of being in the back seat of the van, catching her eyes in the rear-view mirror. No, that couldn't be right – there was no rear-view mirror. I felt a shock that was like the ending of the paralysis dream.

I was the first to go back down. The other two lingered there for a while, and I busied myself stripping the damp bark off the branches. I used up as much wood as I was able to, as if this were the last night, but leaving the cot bars to one side. It would be sacrilege to burn them.

I started on the wine, and they seemed to sense that, because down they came before I'd taken the bottle from my mouth.

'I found this today and thought you'd like it.' He was extending his hand to me, in it a slim hardback book with a milk-white cover. I recognized the style of the painting on it. It was a Picasso harlequin I hadn't seen before, a young boy, his son I imagine.

'Thanks,' I said. 'Where were you today?'

'At home.'

I flicked through the book with a smile on my face, stopping at an image of a bull's head.

'What is it?' Árab asked. 'Well?'

'Nothing.'

Later, in the same improvised bed of the previous night, when the wine stopped feeling warm inside me and my stomach hurt, I irritated Ziggy and Árab by pulling the blanket down to let some cool air blow over me. Ziggy was eager for conversation; Árab's eyes were summoning evil presences from the dark corners of the room. I was between the two of them, groaning and pulling the blanket off their shoulders. They tolerated me because my suffering was comic.

'People are only going to be glad to see me again,' Ziggy said. 'I don't want to rub it in, but you two ...' Árab shifted about but said nothing, and I began to think that he was silent from worry – worry that his fate was being decided elsewhere. I stopped glancing over at him and fixed my eyes on Ziggy's mouth in the firelight as her monologue went on, till gradually her words fell away. I was convincing myself that it was a scream I was looking at, but mentally I had to concede that her lips weren't panicking. There was a suppressed excited smile, twisting her lips slightly, that came and went. Her lips were taunting us or amusing us, but not comforting.

'Your jaw dropped at one of the paintings in the Picasso book,' Árab said when he eventually spoke. 'Which one?'

He was so far from my own train of thought that what he said seemed senseless to me. Ziggy joined in, in a taunting way. I thought back to the book and said: 'Not a painting. You know the sculpture of the bull's head, made from a saddle and handlebars.'

'Yes?' Ziggy said expectantly.

'That was the end of the sentence,' I said. Árab and I laughed and Ziggy pounded me with her fists, then pulled the blanket completely over to her side. We grappled it back, and she lay as still and silent as she could, for as long as she could.

I was looking into the dark, at the shapes swimming in air, and a series of faces appeared and disappeared, with the shapes superimposed on them like domino spots. A line, 'The blood-pearls spangle your face', floated into my head. Normally it frightened me, this cartoon-show before sleep: not now.

'I can smell that incense-smell again, that you said was damp,' I said. I looked over at Árab: his eyes were just as wide as before.

'How many nights will we be here?'

Ziggy had raised herself onto her elbows, to say the thing we had avoided saying.

'Are you missing somebody?' Árab asked. I was alerted to something hidden in his words.

'We thought you'd gone back this morning,' I said to Árab. 'And we were going to stay on. You don't have to worry about us.'

'You thought that?'

'Yes.'

'You had to know that that was impossible.'

'Don't say that. It's going to have to be possible,' Ziggy said. 'I'm sorry I asked.'

Ziggy woke me in the night and gradually I became aware that my skin was touching flesh. She was touching me and making sure I was excited, every now and then moving up to whisper 'Ssh!' in my ear. I kept still. Now she was on her side, pressed close, rubbing her body against mine slowly. She pressed her forehead into my cheek until I thought my cheekbone would break, and let go. She said something that I missed, but my voice was somewhere else and I said nothing. She was lying on her front with her face turned away.

Ziggy's breathing grew heavy almost instantly, but it was a long time before I could sleep again.

23

The first shock was to be awake and be too floppy to act a part in the drama. It was like this when you were coming round from being under ether, perhaps: a soundless quality to the action, despite the loud soothing and consoling going on. I was being sick over the charred fire, having been whirled out from bed. The sick was good and returned me to myself. This scraping dry of your throat and insides is absolute proof of existence. The two concerned figures standing over me looked absurd.

'Árab,' I was saying and reaching out to him through a haze, 'I have to tell you my dream.' His face was impassive, perhaps he was shaking his head a little: I sensed some disapproval. 'Oh no,' I said, 'have I wet the bed?' It was all I could think of.

'With your sick, yes. Just lie still, for Christ's sake.'

Ziggy was beside me, pushing the hair back from my forehead.

'I've always wanted somebody to do that,' I said. I was playing on my condition now, whatever it was, and playing it for laughs. 'Towels and plenty of hot water,' I shouted out. I could see Ziggy smiling, but Árab's face was still a blank, and very white, just as on the night of Theresa's party.

Ziggy was saying my name until I focused on her and showed that I was listening. 'You were ...' She looked over at Árab, for confidence or for him to supply the word. 'Convulsing,' she said.

I knew what that word meant. Why were they not interested in the dream? I mentioned it to them again.

'We want to hear it,' Árab said, his face close to mine. 'But you have to listen to what we've got to say first. All right?' He was pronouncing his words carefully.

It was Ziggy who explained things to me, after I had sat up and wiped my mouth and drunk some of the mineral water Árab produced. Where had he conjured that from? It would be like him to have a secret stash of supplies.

... She had woken up to the sound of a baby whimpering and thought she was in a dream for a few seconds, but the whimpering was coming from me. She shook me to wake me, but it didn't work, and she woke Árab instead. His idea was to pinch my earlobe hard, and they thought this was a success, because I stopped whimpering and said Árab's name, very slowly – 'scarily', he said. Then I stiffened and my body seemed to arch, before the thrashing began. It lasted two minutes, maybe five. When I came round was when I was sick.

'I thought Brobyn on the bridge was bad,' Árab said. 'But this was a hundred times worse.'

'Árab,' Ziggy said with feeling. I understood. *Not now. Be quiet.*

I mapped out my future in my imagination as an invalid, but I was still not disconcerted enough. Nothing could tear me away from the dream.

'Well, all right, tell us,' Ziggy said, holding on to

Árab's arm and ushering him down beside her. His attention was straying.

'Let him light the fire first, it's freezing,' I said. I said it to prove that I wasn't confused. I could still interpret Árab's movements and glances round the room.

'I'll help,' Ziggy said.

I sat with my back against the wall and my knees drawn up, contemplating their movements. If what I saw could have been translated into words, it would have been something like 'She's closer to him now'. I had that impression without it being accompanied by feelings of jealousy. Simply understood it: she's gone.

I was not so bad that I couldn't dress myself. Pushing the buttons through the holes of my shirt, even if it felt like writing with frozen hands, was possible. Ziggy and Árab must have got dressed when my mind was away.

They came back and we sat down on the bed. Only a corner of the blanket was soiled, and I was uselessly rubbing a stick over it to clean it. Ziggy took the stick off me and, holding my face in her hands, looked at my eyes in doctor-fashion. She seemed satisfied.

'I have to go back to the beginning for your sake,' I said, looking at Ziggy. 'Árab knows most of it. It's the same dream, Árab, except I pushed it to the end this time. There's someone following me, through the rubble of ...' Actually I wasn't sure, as I retold this part of the dream, if I really had dreamt it just then. Only from the middle of the dream did it seem recent.

The middle part, the slow part with the dying and dead cattle, was identical in feeling but not precise detail. The white horse had become a white bull – white because it seemed sculpted from bone, even if it was alive. The bull had the horse's strangled agony, but it wasn't on the edge of things, with the washing lines and telegraph poles, but in the centre like an immolated beast. The mad eye was pleading with me. I walked across the slabs to the other side, to see if its eye followed me. I think I insulted it, treating it like a painting in a gallery. The eye followed me, though.

Stephen wasn't playing his guitar when I went back inside. He was holding it upright by the neck and standing in the hall, next to the farm painting, and clearly posing, unsmiling, for a photograph. He had long hair and his head was tilted to one side. There was nobody with a camera, nobody else there at all except me, and I realized that he was posing for his part in the dream, as if he was saying: 'This is how you will remember me.'

I had the same uncertainty on the top landing as to which room to enter. It wasn't as if there was a space for my mind to remember in: I didn't think 'Gran will be there, holding open the red curtain.' But there was enough of a feeling of *déjà vu* for me to try to cheat fate. I did it not by opening a different door, but by opening the same door. Unexpectedly, the identical scene lay before me.

I knew now what followed, and I tried to turn and run before I had to witness her signalling to my murderer, but though I was quicker this time, I still caught it out of the corner of my eye.

There was no sense of that futility in running that happens in dreams. I moved fast out of that dark, dead room, and had crossed the hall to my mother's bedroom. My hand's pressure on the door-handle was misdirected somehow, and as the door opened, the handle slapped back up with a bang. It was perhaps this that gave my mum her startled look.

It was more than startled, and I could feel the hairs on my neck begin to rise. She was sitting on the cushioned stool at her dressing-table mirror, and it was in the mirror that my eyes met hers. They were red from crying that had gone on so long that they were bone-dry now. They frightened me, with their accusing look. Then there was something else.

Out of the white closet. It was a voice, very deep, submarine, a man's voice. There must be a man hidden in the closet that was too small to contain a man.

Unmistakably he was speaking to me. With that deep voice. He was saying: 'It's all right, it's all right, it's all right, it's all right.'

• • • • • • • • • • • • • • • • •

Ziggy stroked my forehead again; Árab lit a cigarette and passed it to me. I took the smoke inside, because I appreciated his gesture of sympathy, if that was what it was, and not because I wanted to smoke. More than anything I wanted clean air pouring into my lungs.

'It means something, doesn't it? The dream.'

Árab looked at me as if I was mad.

'Of course it does. You mean you don't know?'

I glared at him. 'It's not an exercise. You don't get good marks for being right. Don't fuck with me.'

'I'm not fucking with you, it's straightforward, the voice is your dad's. It's your dad telling you that it's all right.'

I felt a rising sense of horror.

'It's not as obvious as you say,' Ziggy said. 'Though I suppose you're right.'

'I knew last night you were thinking about him, just from the Picasso book. The bull in your dream and the bull in the book. You don't have to work too hard. It's a father thing. You must know that.'

'I wasn't thinking about him last night.' I knew with a feeling as certain as instinct that he was right: there was no sense in arguing, and to save face a little I said, 'Not consciously.'

'It was what the voices-of-the-dead book was about,' he said. 'You wanted to hear *his* voice. Now you've heard it.'

• • • • • • • • • • • • • • • • •

I suppose I was half-crazed. 'Half-crazed' sounds better than 'unwell'. Whichever, when we traipsed home finally, I had two more nights before I could sleep in my own bed. I spent them in hospital. That was where I made up lines about 'lantern-jawed nurses'. One of the nurses reminded me of Ziggy's sister, Marie. I spoke to her when she was near me and said: 'George Orwell, my father, was treated for TB in this hospital.'

'Really?' she asked.

'No, not really.'

Though it was true that my dad's name was George.

He died when he was thirty-eight years old, from injuries sustained in a road accident. He was on a bike.

It pleased me that Árab had missed the significance of that detail – the Picasso bull being made from a saddle and handlebars. I had missed so much; he could afford to miss that.

24

Ziggy went back to her musician, a matter of weeks later. I was euphoric at first, running from cliff-edge to cliff-edge on one of my last visits to the glen with Árab. I told him it was a fresh start. I felt as though I had died and gone back to the same life. I was incredibly sensitive to suffering for months afterwards, and cried over a butterfly that had been shut in the toilet. Árab was already looking forward to the magic mushrooms reappearing. I'd had my fill of them. We argued over Van Gogh, and if he painted the way he did because of a drug extracted from foxgloves. I said he didn't, and got a book of his letters to his brother (I was spending a lot of time in the library) which I said proved it. Then we argued about why we were arguing. Then I called him a liar. He walked away from me, across the rugby field at the edge of that part of the glen, and it was the end of our friendship.

I worked at my poems in the isolation that followed, and they became a lot tighter, but my imagery dried up and I found new poems harder to write. Mostly I had one theme, that of having to choose between two women. The two women in my imagination back then were Ziggy and a girl I dreamt up and called Anna. I had one that started:

> With a kind of dreaming instinct
> Your calm animal eyes reflect
> A landscape where thorn-trees are,
> Where you go wading through moonlight.

It was elegant, I suppose, but Anna wasn't in it. Her bristling presence might have been in the short Ziggy poem I wrote:

> She caught the angle of my eye
> And with levelling voice said
> *The moon is not infallible*;
> I said *I don't believe that.*

There was a lot of moonlight – many moons.

I propped the Rousseau print in its black frame on the mantelpieces of wherever I went after that. The painting reminded me of my first night in the glen, that mystical night, when I walked with Árab out of the close-packed darkness of the forest, into the clearing with its full moon.

I split with Ziggy before I split with Árab, but I did go out with her once more. She phoned me and invited me over, and for a day or two I thought it might all be beginning again. We went to a Glasgow cinema to watch David Bowie in Nicolas Roeg's *The Man Who Fell To Earth*. 'You get to see Bowie's balls in it,' she said with much laughter. She told me on the bus home, over the cigarette we shared, 'I expected you to try to put your arm round me. I thought about it. I wouldn't have pushed you away.' I tried placing my hands everywhere that might work for me on the rest of the way back, but she wasn't interested: her mind was made up.

There was a lot of grief for my mum before I left

school. I was almost never there, and she was constantly being kept informed. Árab was suspended for one month. He won notoriety and new friends; though, in fairness, I had never been his friend exclusively. I had made him mine exclusively. As Ziggy once said: 'Error.'

• • • • • • • • • • • • • • • • • •

It doesn't end for me, though, that whole time, with the Bowie film or Árab disappearing over the horizon. As a matter of fact, it ends earlier, maybe a month after I left hospital and went home. Once more I should have been at school and wasn't: I spent the entire morning and afternoon in the same spot, at a desk in the library reading Kafka's *America* in one sitting. I saw the book recently in an edition that had a futurist-type painting on the cover, with one prominent wheel. I'm almost certain it was the same cover. I still wasn't aware enough back then to recognize that images of wheels conjured my dad for me. I had been nervous that day, and I had to imagine that I was clamped to the chair. Reading the whole book through made my mind feel whole. At about four thirty I stood up and let the pins and needles eat away at my legs.

When I walked outside I was startled. The sky was blue-black with evening coming on, but everything else was white. There was almost a foot of snow lying, and a few flakes still falling. It acted like a lullaby on me. I pictured – that's not it, I *remembered* – standing almost eye-level to the window-sill, distressed, waiting one more evening for him to appear home from work. I look up into the cage of boughs and suddenly it's snowing. I hear my own laughter ringing in my head.

I walked the whole way home and at one point I heard another voice, and saw his face: that fat boy smirking and saying 'His dad's in America with his bird', a senseless remark I never understood. It made a kind of sense to me for a few moments, then; and I let the Kafka-snow land on my face.

We heard thunder in the west:
an ancient symbol was sinking down.
We were young then, in the forest.

Didn't we invent the colour green?
Soft crumbling crutches in the sky,
telegraph poles flecked the scene.

We hated pylons, their slow buzz.
Insects we could sympathise with,
and the moon's scorpion claw was over us.

We invented everything, the dragon-trees,
the mushrooms like sea-horses in the fields,
and a real horse in one field, a gypsy's.

**

Branches stand for desire.
You drag them through a clearing.
You make the night-fire.

You find me in your Spain.
You make the night-fire.
You make my dead walk again.

from In The Forest

Peaches and Monkeys' Tails

'I want *grape*fruit. Grapefruit *and* cornflakes.'

He quickly picked out her straw-coloured hair. There was enough silence, and not too much distance between their tables, for him to hear without effort. The either-or principle of breakfast courses was being politely hissed by the landlady, and again the girl was rebelling.

'But you wouldn't even *like* grapefruit, darling,' the woman sitting beside her said, with much more warmth (her mother, clearly) and as little success.

When the girl threw a napkin to the floor – she'd had to pick it out of a glass first – and scraped back her chair, he was hoping that her passionate exit would take her round his side of the table where she would have to squeeze past. He liked seeing her angry: her face had extra little bulges then, over the eyes and round the mouth, as though pockets of air had got under the skin. But no. The landlady's thin lantern-face stretched with horror. The girl was making a beeline for the door, upsetting bags, chairs, even his mother's surreptitiously slipped-off shoes.

His father snapped at him for laughing.

A sensitive soul, he ate what was left of his toast glumly, wordlessly, but when his dad's camera was passed to the nearest other dad and he and his brother were told to smile, dutifully he opened his mouth. He knew very well what he would contribute to the photograph: an unease inside the brown prickly crew-neck, a slight blush, a merciless fringe. His mother pressed a new 50p piece into his hand and he was off. But he was sorry to go when he caught what happened next: his father's voice inviting the wild girl's mother to sit with them.

Out in the hall, he joined in at first with the excited running up and down stairs, but he was older than these children and they let him know that, withdrawing like winkles into their shells when he clumped by. It wasn't last year any more. He thought of the girl and imagined her screaming into a pillow in her room ... or perhaps she didn't do this?

His father must have locked their door. There was a communal toilet in the landing: he'd take revenge for being locked out by not washing his hands.

The sun dazzled him briefly as he stepped outside, so that the girl's face took some time to come into focus. She was on the doorstep, bunching up the loose skin around her knee, a radio on her lap. He must still have been dazzled, because he found himself greeting her for the first time, and not childishly, but with words he'd heard his parents exchange often enough.

'Do you want anything from the shop? I'm going there.'

She put a hand to her forehead as if she were about to salute him; under it, her face looked quizzical, then broke into a smile. It was the longest-lasting smile he'd ever seen.

'What's your game?' she said at last.

Without having exactly misheard her – he'd heard all right, but not understood – he answered by saying his name. Her smile turned into laughter and she extended a limp hand, saying: 'Mine's Jane. Pleased to meet you. I don't want anything from the shop, thanks.'

He almost skipped along the street, he was so happy. The wind blowing the seaside detritus in small circles also peppered his eyes with sand, and as he neared the corner shop he rubbed his eyes and stopped to spit, looking back across the front gardens to see if Jane could see him here; she could, but she wasn't watching. He wheeled the rack of postcards round till he got to the dirty ones. When the shop door blew open he took it as his cue to go inside. He bought sherbet and chocolate mice, making sure there were a few 2ps in his change: he would use them in the machine outside. He knew what he wanted. There was a one-in-five chance of getting the capsule that he'd give to Jane.

And his luck was in. The first that dropped down

contained a ring.

The long street was only a space for him to rehearse in: how he was actually to do this, hand her the ring, when even in his own imagination he was too actorly. The moment would have to decide.

She had stripped down to T-shirt and bikini bottoms when he saw her next, despite the cold, with the clothes she had taken off underneath her on the step. They were spread out, he thought, to make a seat for two; but he thought wrong, and she pushed him off in amazement at his boldness, which privately she had to admire. He was confused.

'You can have this,' he said, producing the half-clear, half-purple plastic pod, with the yellow ring rattling inside. 'It's for a girl.'

'Keep it and give it to your girlfriend, then,' she said, 'if you've got one.' She caught a shadow of fear crossing his face: it was enough to make her laugh again, but she stopped abruptly, to turn the radio up. 'I love this one,' she said. He'd heard it before, liked it thoughtlessly: now at full volume it made him feel as though his bones were rattling like the ring inside him.

Walkin' on the beaches
Lookin' at the peaches

Still sitting, half-lying back, she wriggled a staccato dance whose movements he imitated, though with some reserve.

'Do you know what the song's about? Do you?' she asked.

It *had* struck him as odd, the idea of peaches growing on a beach, but then he'd never been abroad on holiday.

'Peaches are a lady's, you know ... ' she said, casting her eyes down to the logo on her T-shirt. 'My, you know ... '

He looked at the flatness she indicated, but understood what she meant.

'Bumps?'

'*Breasts.*'

She sighed with mock-exasperation, closing her eyes against the pale sunlight once more. He would have to work quickly now.

'Your mum is sitting with my mum,' he said, 'and my dad and my brother.'

'What?'

'If they're still there,' he said, more cautiously. 'Your mum sat in my chair when you stormed out the room.'

'I didn't *storm out.* Why would she want to … ? I'm going to see.'

She went barefoot over the red stones to the bay window, too interested to bother about him walking in her shadow. If he stood on tiptoe he was almost her height, so long as she bent over slightly to see inside. And he was vindicated: the four of them still sat there, talking in the empty dining room, his father especially, John with his listening adult face on, and his mother with a pained look that made him want to be in there tugging her sleeve. Then Jane said the most extraordinary, horrific thing.

'Your dad better not be interested in my mum.'

• • • • • • • • • • • • • • • • •

They never let you do what you want, even when what you wanted wasn't *bad*. He was allowed to go by himself to the end of the street, and the only thing that could kill him after that (he'd known how to cross a road *years* ago) was a tram. Trams went about two miles an hour.

So he'd have to wait for John to decide when to go out, and John only wanted to go to amusement arcades, to talk to girls (which after all *he* could do now) and lose money – though never all his money. John didn't even want him around, he could tell. He'd end up by himself, flicking windows over unlit numbers at bingo.

It was troubling, what she'd said.

He watched his mum and dad talking. He'd heard

his dad called 'a smooth operator' by his mum many times, but always in the context of laughter, teasing. He understood the pun, once it had been explained to him: his dad was a surgeon; surgeons operated. He also understood what a 'bedside manner' was, and that his dad had it – it was town-renowned. But he didn't mean anything by it: how many times had he heard his dad speak on the phone, and you'd think he was speaking to a long-lost sister in Australia, and then he'd come off the phone and you'd actually hear him *swear* – under his breath, maybe, but you'd hear the words. If Jane's mum was so stupid she fell for it ... well, it wasn't his dad's fault.

The talk was about Jane suddenly. They weren't arguing at all; they agreed about everything.

They were so selfish they could only ever think of the trouble children caused *them*, not the other way round. Jane was right to demand grapefruit. 'Poor woman,' his mum said. Poor Jane, more like. Now that they couldn't just spell out words when they didn't want him to understand, they used long, complicated ones. Like the one his dad had just said, which he could tell was a word that only surgeons and doctors ever used. 'Poor woman,' his mum said again.

• • • • • • • • • • • • • • • • •

He was amazed to see her. He'd opened the door before John could get to it, and it was Jane, dressed differently, but still a whirl of colours. His disappointment when she looked past him towards his mother was short-lived: she was asking if he could come out, for a little while; just to the beach.

He.

Of course they would say no, especially since it was Jane. Hadn't he just listened to their condemnations of her? But something miraculous occurred, as it did from time to time when he least expected it: his parents said yes. John seemed happy too. They were all acting, in fact, as if they *liked* this girl.

His mother went out of her way to prove to him that she'd not changed her nature completely – that would be frightening – by stipulating that it must only be to the beach that they went, and only the stretch adjacent to these streets. And for an hour at most. And she must bring him back.

The awkwardness he'd felt earlier was now hers to feel, and on the way to the beach she played down the whole asking-him-out affair: she'd been bored, she said (and yawned); her mother was no fun these days. At the zebra crossing she offered him her hand, but he rejected it: either she held hands the whole way or not at all. How much suffering this rejection caused him!

Twice his shoelaces came undone; the second time she bent over and tied another – double – knot. He would have stopped this too, but he felt pleasantly paralysed for a few moments. Jane rested on one of the long iron bars that fenced off the beach.

'I was wrong about your dad before,' she said. 'Sorry. It's just that he's a doctor or something – isn't he? – and my mum's not been well. That's what they talked about. I don't know what's wrong, I think it's ...' She looked at his taut, expectant face. 'Do you know what periods are?'

'Yes,' he said.

'Really, you do? I'm impressed. What are they?'

'You get them in secondary.'

'Well, *yes* ... '

'You get six in the morning and four in the afternoon after lunch.'

'What?'

'Like two periods of chemistry, then two biology ... '

'Oh my God,' she said, covering her face with both hands. She managed not to laugh this time.

As if in answer to her prayer, something distracted them. A man appeared with a monkey and set up in comically-fast time a stall with a tropical backdrop.

'You,' the man said, panting, 'want your picture taken with Charlie?'

'We've no money,' Jane said. It was a small lie. He'd seen his mum put a note into her hand. 'For an ice cream,' she had said.

'That's all right, you can play with Charlie and I'll *pretend* to take your photo. It attracts custom quicker.'

She looked at her young friend's eager eyes (her own were bright too).

'We'll do it if you give us a photo for free. You may as well check everything's working OK.'

The man's grin exposed a mouth full of bad teeth. 'I could cut myself on you,' he said. 'Come on then.'

The monkey seemed interested only in playing with Jane's hair, but it did sit happily in his lap. He was shy of it at first, not shy of its animal nature so much as the oddness of its appearance, got up as it was in T-shirt and dungarees. He watched Jane's smiles and cooing and laughter; her infectious self-forgetfulness overcame him, so that when the man approached with the photo drying in his hand, he was genuinely shocked by the relaxed image of himself captured in it.

'Now bugger off,' the man said, in a friendly voice, and lifted Charlie from around Jane's neck. A queue had already formed at the stall. One boy made a thrusting karate movement as they passed, shouting 'Ha! *Mung*-kee!' Jane giggled.

He was now wondering excitedly if there would be donkeys on the beach; Jane would easily have enough money for donkey rides. He took her hand to urge her onwards, but she was enthralled by the photograph, looking, waving it in the air, looking again. Only the sensation of sand running over the exposed parts of her feet brought her back to him.

It looked as though the money would have to be used for ice cream.

She trusted him with the money, and watched as he ran awkwardly to the wheel-less ice cream van. Then she took the inexpensive shades from her back pocket, wishing that she'd worn them for the photograph, and sat on the sand. He was soon in conversation with another boy over there: they seemed to be comparing arms, then legs. It was surprising, really, how forward he could be, for someone so shy. She waved to him as he pointed her out.

He came back carrying the cones judiciously, with the other boy in tow. This boy was nearer her own age, she realized suddenly, and quite tall; his skin was a pleasant colour.

'What do you say, goosebumps or goosepimples?'

'What? Goosepimples,' she said

'*See.*'

'Hello, I'm Peter,' the bronzed boy said. 'I've been trying to tell him there's no right or wrong word, it depends where you live what word you say.'

'Absolutely. I'm Jane.'

He saw that he'd made a mistake; that, the dispute settled, Peter wasn't going to go away. She was blushing, which he *knew* was a bad sign, while Peter talked exaggeratedly about rollercoasters. If Peter asked them to go along with him, it would spell disaster: he was too small to get on those rides.

She was showing Peter the photo; they laughed conspiratorially, and she blushed deeper. It was a good photo, surely they weren't laughing at him? No, it was something to do with Charlie's tail, apparently. Apparently, tucked between his legs, it looked like ... Jane said one of those surgeon's words.

His ignorance only amused them. 'I had to tell him about periods before,' Jane said. This betrayal – a barefaced lie – was the last straw. He wiped his ice cream-smeared hands on her top.

'You!' she said, clutching his hands and pulling them to her mouth. He winced, screwing up his face for the expected bite, but all she did was lightly place her lips on his skin and leave them there. He was more confused than ever.

'I want to go home,' he said. 'I mean to the ...'

'I know what you mean ... I'll have to take him back.'

'Will you come back here?' Peter asked.

'I don't know, I don't know. Just let me take him back first.'

They crossed the road into the street. He stopped at the 2p machine and searched his pockets, while she waited impatiently. He looked at all the capsules through the thick plastic, stalling by pretending to consider which one he wanted, tracing a finger over them as though he were reading.

'I'm allowed to be in the street by myself,' he said. 'Remember this morning?' And he kept up the war until she surrendered.

'If you're *sure*,' she said unhappily. 'Give your mum all the change that's left. I've counted it.'

She retraced her steps and his stomach sank. He didn't move from the machine for quite some time, and when he did, he returned to the promenade also, but without looking for her. Instead he allowed himself to be carried with the crowd, vaguely in the direction of the Tower. He must have gone for miles and miles, he thought, and still he was unafraid. He would pick up the stride of the two girls – women, he supposed they were – walking in front.

Medicine

Yesterday, awkwardly, I waved to her from the tower. She was a field's breadth away at the time and struggling through cowslip. The tower we had for a month. 'We must make the most of this,' she had said, and we did, loving the cool stone, the view of the estuary and the farm. It was not so isolated as you could believe: the town was beyond the wood, and the city just three stations away. The un-Roman road was so winding that it was best to go through fields, but it meant that I could walk along it and exercise enough without meeting people. Everyone should have a month without people. But when a month becomes a year then a decade ... That was also why we were here, for Anna's brother, who'd been alone too long (so we told ourselves) and was now hospitalized. The hospital was in town.

When we heard about Alan I was looking through slides for an exhibition, Anna turning white-faced from the phone with her hand over the receiver, saying 'Alan's sick, mentally,' as though she'd just made the diagnosis herself, and I remember that the slide I had on the light-box was called *Medicine*. I saw instantly that my work was too slick. *Medicine* was an installation, a huge white aspirin on a white wall with images projected onto it, some of the sick and dying; the same set of images was flashed up at an increasing speed until the aspirin turned black and the whole thing started again, meditatively slowly at first. Anna saying that he'd gone into hospital sealed it for me, and I switched off the light-box in self-disgust. I was already taking down my greatcoat and barking at Anna 'Where? Which hospital?' when she said, to an apparition in mid-air possibly, 'No. We have to think about this one.'

That greatcoat seemed almost to be reserved for emergencies. I would grab it down like a comic routine as one casualty followed another, especially this past year. A friend was killed in April, in a road accident. That's *more* than a year ago now. There were complications with Anna's pregnancy. We called our baby Lorca, after the Spanish poet of course – not the name we would have given him if he'd been born. It helped us, reading those brief poems, Lorca's *Suites*, in bed together at night: it seemed to us that they were poems still in the womb, not developed fully but perfect nonetheless. We loved them for that.

After soothing me, Anna was back on the phone speaking to somebody important, speaking very coolly and jotting things down. I went into the kitchen and drank some water, feeling it settle in my stomach as though it were Anna's voice. So I was not to be the rock on this occasion, I thought. Apart from wounded pride I felt relief. Connections of her father secured the tower for us and we moved north, leaving even the car behind, determined to live simply, to walk into town to see Alan (Anna each day, I whenever) and begin to have good dreams again, our telepathic dreams of old.

The tower couldn't keep me secluded forever, and on the third night we ventured out to the White Horse, continuing the dissection of Alan's childhood there. I expect those words convey the tiredness I was experiencing with that subject, but strangely I warmed to it in new surroundings, briefly at least, and the pub's over-ornate fittings, the pungent smell of smoke from the turf fire, even just the name of the pub itself, elevated Alan's sufferings to the mythic plane. Anna recounted her father's harshness towards him when they were young; I couldn't keep my eyes from straying to the horse's head in the crest above the bar, its arresting, tortured appearance.

'I just gave up on him,' she said. She was stretching a little pool of spilt beer into an asterisk shape with one finger and flashing a look up at me occasionally, her eyes beautifully outlined with thin red rims. With her right hand she was obsessively flicking ash from her cigarette, hardly smoking it: we'd both started smoking again, agreeing to say nothing about it. I was drawing slowly and heavily on my cigarette in conscious contrast, a slow, heavy, male presence, in reality half-wanting to tremble and scream and unleash Anna's hysteria.

'I should have intervened more often,' she said.

'You might have had some of it coming your way then,' I said.

'No,' she said. 'Dad doted on me.'

'Anyway you were younger than Alan.'

'Just by a year.'

'Still.'

There were some more circles to go round, but eventually she dropped Alan's name from the conversation. Not that we strayed very far; we were still speaking about childhood, and brothers, mothers, fathers.

The place was dark now, with the sort of light a bedside table lamp gives off. She was prompting me to speak about my father – we had only ever discussed him once – but I was unwilling. 'That was his affair,' I said, enjoying the pun: of course he'd left us all for a woman, one who'd not present him with any more children. They happily or unhappily ran a hotel in Brighton.

'It sometimes feels like I had a sister, Alan could be so girlish.' She was skating out on one more circle and giggling to herself. 'He still talks about how I used to peer over his shoulder at him in mum's mirror and say "You lipstick good." It cracks him up.'

'I know,' I said.

'I know you know,' she said sharply. 'But just let me talk, all right?'

I let her talk and let the silence lengthen after she said 'Those days are well and truly ...' and it wasn't that I let it wash over me. The anxiety that creased her face and the small bursts of laughter that smoothed it out again – I drank it all in.

'Anna,' I said. 'It's a wonderful thing you've done, coming up here. It wasn't a sacrifice for me – if anything I work better in a place like this. I want to go with you tomorrow. I know I've hardly seen Alan, but I love him too, he's so special that I sort of wanted to put off seeing him, like wanting to put off working on something really good, that really means something to me, you know how I do that.'

She simultaneously smiled and stubbed her cigarette out, then felt behind her for her coat. Our empty glasses had sat there a long time. Anna smiled again, as we left, at the barmaid who was reaching up to a shelf underneath the crest.

We walked the road back, not feeling that we had to speak, and once we were in the tower again I laid out all my sketchbooks and paper on the first-level table, convinced that something worthwhile was about to emerge. At three am all I had was a line in my diary: *Of Alan. Brought on father-talk in brown* (the brown was a reference to the pub's wallpaper). I was retreating into my cave, the place where I must wait for new preoccupations. 'Father-talk in brown' dismayed me a little: it was an area of my life I was reluctant to visit.

Anna was sleeping when I got to the top of the stairs. She must have undressed in the dark, as the curtains weren't drawn. The view all the way round from this room was superb in the day but we also knew from our walks just how visible the room was from all sides; maybe only a fox or a sea-bird was watching, but that would be enough for Anna. Or – and I thought this as I looked at her sleeping face – a weight had fallen from her and she was more carefree suddenly.

It was always my intention to visit Alan the next day, but the way my telling Anna worked out, I was going now out of conviction. Like a man of conviction, because I had slept badly, I was up and showered and dressed first. I dressed as casually as I would have for a day at the beach. Surely the hospital wasn't a decrepit Victorian asylum. Lazily I wondered why I hadn't asked Anna about it before.

I picked up Lorca's *Suites* to bring with me, thinking that it was these small pills of madness he needed and not *The Consolation of Philosophy*. He would learn what I had learned, to be sanely mad and keep himself out of these places. I was looking forward to seeing him now and could picture his wide grin and surreally wavy black hair. It was true he would be pale, maybe even lost-looking, but not for long. Not with the two of us on form.

Anna was in a thin summer dress and we held hands on the way. She made no attempt to prepare me for an experience I might find daunting, in fact she chatted happily, and this was encouraging. It turned out that the hospital was at the opposite end of town from the White Horse and *was* old. 'Annexe' was written in stone above one door.

The old imposing façade was just that. Alan was housed in a small hostel in the compound beyond. I counted seven buildings in the compound and noticed two of the names that were displayed so prominently, Taylor-Wolff and Tyler Fox. Alan was in Fox.

Which were his first words to me. He lifted his hand weakly to shake mine, and said: 'I am inside the fox. As you see.' Then he said, pointing to the woman standing over him, 'Let me introduce my friend.' I had been so engrossed in studying Alan's face as I approached him, held by the mischief playing in his eyes, that I'd not looked properly at this woman. I'd vaguely thought she was a nurse, but looking at the angular and tormented features of her face I could see that she was a patient too. She was dressed all in grey, was barefoot, not unattractive. She was now holding the hand Alan had pointed with. Anna leant into me.

'Alan, it's good to see you,' I said.

'He says it's good of him to see you,' the woman said and laughed – they both did.

'Alan,' Anna said with feeling.

We made small talk, still standing round him uncomfortably, with the woman in grey chuckling to herself occasionally. I noticed that Alan would squeeze her hand when she laughed, and so fiercely that I thought his strength must have returned to him. I asked him if he could walk, outside with us, if that was allowed.

'I've not been sectioned, you know,' he said.

'No, of course not.'

I recognized a monkey puzzle tree in the wonderfully exotic gardens, but little else. It would have been useful to be able to talk endlessly about flowers and trees and prevent the conversation from drying up. I was angry that Anna was silent.

Alan had found a garden seat, and the woman – whom Alan never did introduce – took up her presumably customary position beside him.

'You're living near here now, I believe,' he said.

'Yes, for a month. Anna must have told you about our tower.'

'Yes, your tower,' he said. He found something amusing in this. 'You didn't up sticks for my sake, did you?'

'No,' I said, then, because it was the truth, 'Yes.'

'We didn't *burn* our house down then come here,' Anna said, touching his arm. It was a relief to hear her speak.

'Of course not ... I burned down my house to come here. Starting with the top storey.'

'Alan.'

I understood what he meant. His friend was shaking with laughter. I couldn't stand it.

'It's good that you found a friend,' I said, glaring at him, then her, then him again. 'I thought it must have been lonely where you were.'

'It must be lonely where you are,' he said sharply.

'What do you mean? You mean the tower.'

'Of course, the tower.'

His friend was whistling a tune that only much later I identified. It fitted grotesquely the situation, a madwoman whistling a nursery rhyme, beside the ridiculous hothouse-looking flowers, while I looked on and sweated. Anna was as cool as stone, and as silent. I had taken her hand and was walking her away from them.

'You're not helping,' she said when the distance was discreet.

'*You're* not helping.'

'You amaze me. This is my fourth time here and the first like this ... Look, I know that awful woman is a pain, but they're inseparable. It must be a good thing. The doctors ... '

'What is it you want me to do?'

'Be natural with him.'

'Be natural. Alan and that woman have it in for me. Tell me you can see that.'

'You're mad,' she said, and we stared, angry and frightened, at each other for a moment too long. 'You're mad with me,' she said softly. 'Let's go back, at least give Alan the book you brought.'

I took the Lorca from my inside pocket and fanned the pages out under my nose. That sweet smell again: I wanted to keep the book. But I strode across and held it out to Alan and then put it in his lap with a few words. I smiled hard and tried to smile with my eyes. The pupils of his eyes were much too big, I thought, the irises too deep a blue. The mischief had gone out of them.

I accompanied Anna more often, even as my desire to shun the place grew, each visit beginning in the hostel and proceeding to the gardens and returning to the hostel again, until a dinner gong banged our farewell. Alan was free to step outside with us, or stay over at the tower, but he seemed to love entrenching himself in hospital routine. The grey woman, as I liked to refer to her with Anna, even after learning her name, was not always got up in grey, though she was always shoeless. She was always by his side. After two weeks she stopped laughing.

Alan reserved a special grin for me, perfected over those weeks, which I took to be a symptom of his condition. It was lopsided, unfriendly but masquerading as friendly (it deceived Anna). I was growing used to it; we were entering our last week here and I told myself that it had lost its power over me, soon I would be leaving it behind. Anna had arranged things to enable her to see Alan again, but I was going to be wrapped up in new work, busy in my studio, with one or two good friends dropping by. I had an idea for an installation I'd call *White Car.*

What was to be my final visit began with comedy. The flat roof of the tower had let rain in during the night and I woke up damp down my left side. It was Anna, dry as a bone herself, who found it funny, until I coughed and there was something odd about the sound of it. Anna wanted to get a fire started and sit me at it while she saw Alan, but I was desperate to go, with the sort of euphoric edge I used to feel on the last day of school. We compromised and I agreed to warm myself and set out later. It was a chance to summon all the disparate elements of the past month, to fuse them, so to speak, mentally in the flames.

I left the tower with my mind crackling and almost skipped to the hospital. I felt like picking all the poppies from the verges. The colour red was forcibly present in me, and I thought, 'This is a red letter day.' I pictured an 'R' painted red hugely on a black background and understood that I wasn't a fake, that the art which came out of me wasn't fake.

I wish I could have kept this in mind throughout the onslaught to come. The first person I saw was Anna, who met my smile with a panicked look, the look I hoped never to see again. She was opening doors in the corridor ahead of me, trying to alert somebody, I thought, to whatever had happened to Alan. I was wrong. I saw soon enough: it was the grey woman, lying next to a pot of honeysuckle, at the end of a fit. The relief I felt was like pleasure and Anna must have caught that in the split second that I stood over the body, smiling, maybe, and inactive. Now her look wasn't panic but the distrust she'd shown me after our friend's cremation, when we'd lost the cortège of cars that was heading for the 'reception' and I suggested we leave it at that. Her grieving required her to talk to people I'd happily miss.

She seemed to spit out that look.

I moved swiftly then and rolled the woman onto her side just as a man not in a uniform pulled my shoulder gently back and took my place. Anna was speaking too rapidly at him. I thought about Alan.

'Alan,' I said to her for the sixth time.

'I don't know. He walked off. You look for him.'

His bed and the armchair in the TV room were empty. Haar was sweeping the grounds outside. I thought I should check the grounds anyway, and sure enough he was there, standing, inspecting flowers, roughly pulling the blossom down or up to his face.

'I thought you wouldn't be coming today,' he said.

'Didn't Anna say?'

'Oh, she said you would be along later, but I didn't expect you. You look pale.'

'I seem to have caught something. Your friend, shouldn't you be with her?'

'I avoid those sorts of scenes. Look at this beauty.'

'That's a crocus, isn't it? I nearly ate one as a boy. I was lucky, they're poisonous. My mother stopped me,' I said, the memory returning. 'I could eat primroses though.'

He said after only a few seconds, 'It's lucky, you said. You ate the primrose. As a child, and not. The poisonous crocus.'

'Very good.'

'Spoiled by the fact that this is not actually a crocus. These petals are edible. Here, have some.' He held out his hand, daring me to eat.

'I'm past the stage of eating flowers now,' I said, and his response – to put the petals in his own mouth instead – was as I expected. It was like that with Alan, he impressed you, spontaneously composing verses that never saw the light of day, and depressed you in turn, with his childish intensity of glaring and posturing.

'I think I'll go in out of this,' I said walking off, but then I heard him say, with a pathos that kept me next to him:

'Stay with me here.'

We looked silently, with contentment, at the flowers, and I thought it was going to be all right. I thought *he* was going to be all right. There was the coldness of his attitude towards his friend to consider, but secretly I shared it. He had humoured her, a grey, nervously laughing presence, almost an absence. That was it: she was an absence of woman.

'You've disappointed me,' he said. Here we go, I thought sadly – the dip on the rollercoaster.

Mechanically I said: 'I have? How?'

'This month. No, longer than that. But this month.'

'How exactly?'

'I've not formulated my thoughts on it. It's not the way I proceed. You understand me?'

'It's a quality I admire,' I said. 'One of many – in you, I mean. You'll think I'm warding off whatever criticism's coming my way. I'm not. I admire you. But the brutal fact is, you're here, and that means something.'

'It means: here comes a stupid poet. Always cries about something in his head ... Sorry, I'm quoting, it's a bad habit.'

'Words are more your thing than mine,' I said.

'Well, *there's* something I admire about *you*.'

'Thank you.'

I imagined that his appreciation would combine with forgetfulness and that I'd heard the last about disappointing him. He looked at me with the usual intensity.

'I thought I'd spurred you into action, collapsing my life this way, and I was pleased to hear you had rented out the tower. I see now that all that was my sister's doing. I've followed your regress over the years, even ordered catalogues from Germany and elsewhere, and yet I thought if I had you to myself, in an isolated mountain cabin, or a tower of my father's business partner – as it turned out – I could shake something real out of you, really startle you into ... '

What could I say? Shout out ridiculously, 'I can be

passionate!' Tell him about taking down my greatcoat?

'This *is* madness, Alan. I wanted not to use ...'

'Save it for the birds. You're not getting out of this. I've tracked you down now.'

I was seriously gauging how dangerous he might be. 'You weren't with me in the tower,' I said, foolishly. 'You speak as though you had planned everything, as though you were God.'

'You'd like to believe that. Then you could go running in there for assistance. Why don't you listen?'

'I'm listening. But I have a chill and it's raining.'

'You should have said. We can go inside.'

There was nobody in the dormitory at Tyler Fox – the *ward*, as I referred to it in my head now. Call a spade a spade. I misread a No Smoking sign as No King, laughed at my mistake, laughed again to think that in this madhouse here I was, for all the world laughing at nothing.

Alan went into his chair and I stretched across one corner of the bed and picked at the blue blanket. He spoke through the prism his hands made, sometimes touching his lips like a child.

'There were three phases to your work, as I see it. Your white phase was about restriction, self-imposed. You were closing the shutters and walking the bare floorboards of your room. Preparing the holy ground. The whiteness was illumination or a fridge, it didn't matter; you yourself couldn't decide whether you were being hygienic or merely spiritual. It was interesting, though. It was a matter of priming the canvas, as I saw it, before the real work began, and it looked as though it was about to begin. You married Anna during this phase. I had no objection.'

'Phase the second?' I said without flinching.

'The second phase was your red phase. You were in a larger room now, you needed a sturdy pair of ladders to get round it, and you slopped the red paint on at first but in the end you spread it a little thinly – more than a little thinly, in fact. And there were precious few pieces of furniture in the room. You were following your blood here, a good Lawrentian, but you forgot to leave your room, silly. You actually titled one piece ... I'm sorry, I'm not laughing ... titled it *Matador*. I couldn't wait for this phase to pass. But when your final phase came I realized I could wait. I could have waited a long time.'

'I'm supposed to be recognizing myself in all this. This is interesting. I thought your thoughts were unformulated.'

'I call your last phase – and I suspect it is your last, unless you are to get on the roundabout once more, revisit White or Red – I call it the mushroom phase. Possibly the *beige* phase. But I prefer mushroom, it makes me think of soup. For two whole years now you have been doing – what? You have made soup. You have sent soup abroad.'

He laughed with his arms wide open, mocking me by offering an embrace.

'Anna is going to leave you now,' he said.

His laughter over, he sat collapsed in on himself. He was the Laughing King at the funfair, I realized, a monstrous inert puppet surrounded by glass, but my money had run out.

A House of Women

We were now what my dad always referred to as 'a house of women', saying it with a look that left you in no doubt what this meant: trouble ahead. Because one thing was certain: my sister (as I hoped to make mum see) really could be called a woman now. She took enormous pleasure in pulling on my old clothes from college days, 'just to wear about the house' – though, going round to see a friend or off to baby-sit somewhere, she would contrive to have no time to change out of them. I was glad to see those old things again; they all should have gone for jumble a long time ago. They fitted her well, and I was happy remembering.

For the fifth consecutive night since I'd come home we ate dinner properly at table, with the television switched off – an effort on mum's part to inspire conversation. She couldn't keep it up, though, and was soon rattling off instructions to Sara – 'Get another serving spoon from the drawer', 'Put a napkin under the gravy boat', 'Serve Catherine first' – which made it clear that, for her, two adults were in the room and someone whose youth marked her out as a skivvy. It infuriated me, since I remembered going through it myself, ten, twelve years back. I talked over mum and told Sara about my new job, the exhibition and all the trouble I put myself to managing the gallery: today, the cabinets had to be repainted and the cabinets and plinths arranged to disguise how few exhibits there were. My intentions were good, but she looked back at me with a bored expression, uncomplainingly got up and sat back down as mum ordered.

I changed tack and poured a little red wine into Sara's glass while mum pretended to be annoyed. We clinked glasses; Sara's clumsy grip on hers meant that the crystal produced a muffled note. I saw a twinkle in her eyes which gave me goosebumps, and I wondered if she was remembering the same thing I was just then: an old boyfriend, Alex, startling us all by making a toast to sex and death in front of Sara. That was in the flat in Camden.

At fifteen, Sara's age now, I would have been more relaxed about accepting a little table wine. I'd maybe be out that same night drinking vodka at a party or in an underpass with some boy. There was more than one boy – it was always serious on their part, not mine. I don't believe I was serious about anything, unless it was the rage I felt at mum's heavy-handedness; not even dad's death penetrated my whimsical armour completely. I remember I dressed very well for his funeral – a few heads were turned. One boy was a constant back then: it was a perpetual non-romance with him. Strange to think now. The squarish glasses he wore are in fashion, or they were a year ago. He taught me metre in poetry in my bedroom one night, chanting the lines of a Thomas Hardy poem. 'Woman much missed, how you call to me, call to me ...' I played dumb then kissed him for the first and last time, one long kiss followed by two pecks on the lips – just to show I understood about metre.

The job really isn't all it was cracked up to be in the literature, but it's a young gallery. Mum's slight shame at my being home is almost justified. She had grown to be a bore, I've heard, talking up my jobs in London and then Amsterdam; seeing the reality of my work close-up must have shorn it of exoticism. Not that she has *seen* any of it, actually. She still floats through life as if blissfully unaware, when God knows she picks up on everything. 'A lolloping daffodil' was how I described her to a girlfriend after one phone call.

I can't put it all down to the old girl, though, this new feeling I've had that my nerves are frazzled. That clunk the glasses made had me imagining my hands around Sara's throat briefly; I screamed inside and pictured the glass shattered. Now I can't explain that. It makes me worry. Where can I go to rest if not here? Through all my travels and hard work and seeing too many faces, I had thought of home as the place to escape to. A trite aphorism about carrying home inside you might be enough for some people. I was both homesick and at home, and I was sick of home.

Christine was the only former friend to try to lure me out of the house at night. I gave reasons then excuses and finally caved in. We met at an old haunt that was a wine bar now, a change we found agreeable since it mirrored the change in us. Out of all the hundreds of crazy things that must have happened to us both, unless we merely dreamt our lives, we had at most two anecdotes which made the other laugh. I know I laughed out of politeness. Christine was reaching down at the side of her chair, picking at something and watching the bar. Then she looked at her hand, disappointed. She had torn off a scrap of wallpaper from around a socket, thinking it dated back to our partying days here. I wrote on it the gallery's number, saying I should have found my own place in a month or two's time and she should call me then. I doubt I could have made it any more plain.

It's true that at one time I dreamt of a glorious homecoming. I even knew which road I would take, making the last mile of its steep hill on foot with battered suitcase in hand. 'Battered' sounds strange, but I would be coming back not to show how much money I had made in the meantime; not even the style I had acquired, though that would be a part of it. I had learnt from many women my age and younger just what marrying and giving birth meant, and if they envied me my freedom to drink and flirt and chat intelligently on the opening nights of exhibitions, I saw perfectly well that they didn't at other times, those evenings when they'd imply I had nothing to go home to and that this explained why I had done so well.

Which was the reason it was so good to meet Claire. By rights we should have been foes: it seemed to be her job as administrator to withold as much money from me as humanly possible and still make the exhibition a success. We got on well and I was more realistic and compromising than in my previous jobs, though I maintained a playful air of deceitfulness so as not to insult her. She, in turn, argued for the inclusion of an African mask among one artist's work. 'Been done before,' I said; she answered with a sweep of the hand, 'So has all this.' (Neither of us had curated the exhibition.) I said she could wear the mask at the opening.

She was, like me, 'between men', but it troubled her more, and more visibly: she wasn't at ease with the workmen, whereas I, who had never had a brother and was without a father for the last fifteen years, chatted to them about their children and about football and helped with crosswords. She darted in and out of the place as though she had something much more pressing to do elsewhere, until lunch-time, which she managed always to extend to a second hour. I didn't lunch with her. I liked Claire but I was a good worker and, besides, I wanted this job done.

Our casual friendship made me feel restless for some reason. I began to go out for walks at night in the surrounding streets (a dog would have taken the bare look off me). I felt dissatisfied and excited at the same time, just like when I was given the present of a car before I could drive – that was how dad trained me for this life. He was perpetually pushing and pushing (it's the reason Sara has turned out differently: she never knew him). One of the first things mum got rid of after his death was the piano, though I still took lessons and was even pretty good. Well, I suppose she thought we couldn't afford lessons now. She could have explained that.

I kept returning on those walks to the swing park at the top of our street. As a girl I would look out from there onto the corrugated factory roofs, knowing that dad was under one of them (I fixed on one, the wrong one, and tried to send messages to him telepathically, keeping my eyes on that same roof as the swing rose and fell). There was a hill of wild grass flowing down to the road; I used to run through it, trying not to scratch the nettle-stings afterwards, and blow dandelion clocks till they were bald. All this was a far cry from the conferences, hotel rooms, early flights. Yet I hadn't changed. Despite what I might say. If dared to, I'd re-carve my initials into the trees around here in a second.

Claire called me at home. She had come up with the idea of us doing publicity jointly – the rounds of a few newspapers and local radio – and thought we could talk ideas over dinner, which she'd cook. Strictly speaking, it was beyond my remit, and I said as much. She was so deflated that I said, 'But I'd love to come for dinner, and it'll give you a chance to persuade me. I'm not doing anything tonight.' She was, I think, reaching into her kitchen cupboards as we spoke.

She lived fairly close to work and not at all in the sort of place I expected. This was a family home, Claire the sole occupant. The kitchen, she said, had once been the lounge, and the old kitchen was now a store room. Just what she had to store that needed a room all to itself was beyond me: I didn't get a tour of the house. A Chinese smell had drifted through to the dining room where I took my place, and yes, the delicate little bowls showed pictures of blue reeds and blue Chinese birds. I uncorked the wine, glad I had made an expensive choice.

It was no surprise to me that the publicity idea went unmentioned. I suggested eating dessert out on the lawn, but Claire shook her head. We discussed men. I told her about my last experience, which was of Alex, when he visited me hoping to re-ignite something between us after splitting from his wife. I made him work for his suppers that long weekend. The night before he left I had a bath, stretched out on the sofa and let him caress me where he wanted without moving. Then – to my shame now – I opened my eyes and said 'What were you doing?' as if I had been asleep. That was all, though I did get into bed with him the next morning. Just to remind myself.

Claire, I sensed, was not at all scandalized by any revelations of mine as I trawled through my past, in fact her face shone with approval, but I noticed her eyes deepen when I berated mum. I felt sure then that her own story must be similar. We were intimate enough for me to ask.

'No, there was nothing like that,' she said. 'She died last year, last summer. The house was paid for.'

'How did she die?'

'I don't know exactly. Well, heart failure. It was more like what they said in the old days, you know, "died of a broken heart". Over a man, but her heart was spent before then.'

'When your dad died.'

'Is he dead? I didn't realize.'

She laughed to ease the tension.

'No, he left after we were born. I had a twin, Terry, he died five years ago. That's what killed mum. You wouldn't have known it, though. She sort of straightened herself out, stopped drinking – not that she was a drunk. Stopped sleeping around, which she did do. This man who left her, called Terry unfortunately, was the first since then. But he treated her like the rest.'

I said some consoling words and made a move which Claire halted. I had thought about making coffee.

'I've not talked about it except to the police and the doctor. It's nothing grisly, I just ... I found her, upstairs. She was rolled up in her eiderdown – which wasn't so strange, she sometimes went for a nap like that. I would have closed the bedroom door on her again, but I saw all her clothes were on the carpet. Not strange, but I'd never seen that before. I went up to look at her. There was a feather from the eiderdown actually lying across her lips. That's a classic test of death, isn't it, that and a mirror? I remember thinking how quaint, as if she'd put it there deliberately, so I'd know. I didn't cry. I didn't.'

I moved round the table. We were wrapped – *wrapped* – in each other's arms, crying ourselves dry, until Claire jumped back. She took me into a long hallway with an old-fashioned staircase and several doors. 'This is the old kitchen,' she said, opening the one door to our right onto a wasteland of toys and clothes and papers. I squealed when I saw a rocking-horse just like mine – it was twenty-odd years since I'd seen it, but I knew.

'Mum kept everything of ours, everything. But all *our* stuff, not dad's or hers.'

'It's fantastic,' I said. 'You just walk in this room and your whole childhood's in front of you.'

'Yes.'

We stayed until it got dark – there was no light bulb in the fitting – and then we had liqueurs in the lounge before I left. But they tasted wrong, grown-up. Claire said so.

For the first time in my life, on the way home, I *wanted* the taxi-driver to speak to me – and of course he did.

Mum had waited up. When I opened the door and put on the hall light I saw her in her nightdress on the top landing, looking ghostly with no light behind her.

'Goodnight, mum,' I said.

'Goodnight, Catherine,' she said.

Jeremy's Home

A new boy was arriving. We had been given his medical chart the week before. That was at the staff meeting. Yvonne had read to us the summary of his eleven years and when she finished Martin said 'Lucky white heather' and we all laughed. I think we felt slightly ashamed. But we were not happy having another placement as it meant all the beds would be full again, and we had bad memories of the last time that happened.

His name, for some reason, was Jeremy. He was Peruvian, so at least he would have some novelty value. I looked forward to trying out my school Spanish on him. In that respect I would have a head start on the others. I could see myself being his special confidante: *un hermano mayor*. Despite the policy of no favouritism, everyone had one or two boys who could do no wrong. After all, Christ had a favourite disciple. Jeremy, I decided in advance, was my John.

Yvonne and I were the two most senior staff on duty. We had delayed bath-time because we didn't want Jeremy's parents arriving to the sight of semi-naked adolescent boys streaming out of the bowl room, but it was getting too near supper-time to delay it any further. Supper-time was not so flexible since evening medication was given then. So, inevitably, the duty car arrived when we were up to our necks in it. Luckily, only Jeremy's mother was with him and she couldn't stay. A new boy's parents meant you had to walk on eggshells usually, but she seemed all right, not too anxious.

It was hard to tell whether Jeremy was sullen and withdrawn or was having several absences. We decided to give him his medication now, in case. He still had said nothing. Instead of the usual cold water I put some orange juice in the cup and brought this and the little eggcup full of tablets to his bed. He was sitting there, a picture of despair.

'Come on, space cadet, here's your tablets.' I tried to raise his chin with one finger, but his neck was rigid. I knelt down and looked into his face, showing him the eggcup. No response. 'I should have shown him the juice,' I thought. I showed him the juice.

'He's absencing bad,' I told Yvonne.

'Come on, Jeremy,' she said. 'Your mum wants you to take these. If you take them you can speak to her on the phone later. There's a good boy, come on.'

This time he looked up.

'Go to hell,' he said.

'It speaks!' Yvonne cried out, laughing and clapping her hands. Three words, beautifully enunciated, and an unmistakable Hispanic timbre. I liked him already.

'Go to hell!' he shouted this time, and hit the cup out of Yvonne's hand.

'You little shit,' she said, annoyed first with him, but then with herself for saying it. 'Look, now your bed's wet. We're going to have to change that duvet ... There's different coloured ones in the store cupboard. Would you like to go with George and pick one?'

We went through the whole repertoire of tricks, but he wouldn't submit. I said I thought we should leave him for now.

'Give him a bath,' Yvonne said sharply, retreating to the office. 'He can have his tablets later. He's not absencing.'

I sat for a long time trying not to appear threatening – said his name quietly once or twice, even hummed a tune. Two of the boys burst in, shouting.

'This the new kid?' one asked.

'His name's Jeremy. He won't take a bath.'

'Hello, Jeremy.'

This boy, the most advanced for his age in the House, was my trump card.

'Are you from abroad? Is he from abroad?'

'He's from Peru, in South America.'

'Cool. Is he an Indian?'

'Don't know. Looks primitive, though. What do you think?'

My trump made an Indian whooping noise. Now Jeremy was making it too, whooping so loud the hilarity brought Yvonne into the dorm. I smiled into her face – foolishly.

'Help me undress him,' she said. We started with the neck of his jumper, pulling it over his head. He held on for dear life and started to kick. I pulled his legs over onto the bed, sat on them, and undid the velcro fastening of his shoes. He curled his toes inside his shoes but I managed to get them off. Then his socks. He scratched my hand as I unfastened his trousers, but his loosened grip meant the jumper was lost. He seemed to sob from somewhere in his stomach. Yvonne couldn't get the T-shirt over his head.

'I'll cut this off if I have to. Christ, he's got a vest underneath.'

His efforts were valiant, but fifteen minutes later he was naked. He stood up, looked at me, and spat. But he went with me to the bathroom and shivered as the bath filled up. Without testing the water, he stepped in and stayed there till I said 'Get out'. I couldn't fetch his pyjamas since that would have meant leaving him in the bathroom, and no epileptic could be left alone there. He walked naked back to the dorm when he was finished. There were pyjamas on the bed. He waited till I left, but I knew he would put them on.

'Get the duty officer out if he refuses his tablets.' Yvonne was buttoning up her coat; I had another half hour before the night staff came in. 'Life's going to be interesting round here again. How's your hand? Put an accident report in anyway. If he keeps it up we'll get him shifted. Have good days off. Doing anything?'

There was the usual high jinks in the dorm, but it quietened down quickly. Jeremy looked asleep, which meant I would have to wake him with his tablets and water.

When I bent over him I saw that he wasn't asleep. He took the tablets, settled back in the bed and stared at the ceiling, his eyes glassy in the light from the office. Then he spoke, very deliberately, just loud enough for me to hear. 'You don't know where it is. I go by plane. You can't get there. You don't know ... '

Excursion

In the end, the sea came into sight. There was a mile or two of swept-back bare trees, incredibly rugged and gnarled, which pointed to the sea's presence before he registered what they meant and turned his head to the left and saw it there. The sand was white. He got off the bus when the landscape was at its most desolate.

He found a path like a Roman road that dissected fields of wheat and was lined with telegraph poles. He was at home here, with the strange-looking creatures that ran along the path, darting into hedges. There were rabbits too, and jackdaws, perhaps oystercatchers, but he wouldn't have known for sure. Even the fences looked green and alive.

At the bottom of the path there was a field with a brown horse and more wind-carved trees. He was drawn to the sparkle of the sea but wanted to linger here, lean against a post and smoke. He smoked two cigarettes in succession, looking at the sky and imagining that he possessed a primitive's ability to read it. The weather would be good, because he wanted it to be.

Depressingly, there was a golf course up ahead: he would have to cross it to get to the sea. He had that feeling, of walking over somebody's grave, as he cut across a green. Before he'd got to the beginning of the grassy dunes he heard a voice.

'You think that nobody can see you, don't you?' It was a young woman, older than him, he thought, as he turned to look at her. Yes, she was two, maybe three years older.

'Don't you?'

He was surprised that she wanted an answer.

'I don't now,' he said. He wasn't sure what to do, if he should move closer to her, or walk ahead, as he had intended, towards the sea. She certainly wasn't going to move. He walked more or less towards her, thinking he could reach the sea in this direction too. He would watch for some moment as he passed her when he would know what was to happen next.

She made the decision for him, asking, when he was a few feet from her, 'Do you want some?' She was holding out a bottle of wine, so it seemed, until she said: 'Don't get excited, it's only water. I put it in this bottle to scandalize the locals. It's easy to do. Why? It doesn't matter. No, it matters, but to me, not to you. Here.' She handed him the bottle. 'If you're staying, maybe we could get some real wine ... You are old enough?'

'Almost, and – yes, if you buy it.'

She pulled a face. Perhaps she was doubtful about him now, about drinking with someone so young.

'I'll give you the money, though,' he said.

'Give me some towards it, later.' She got up to go. 'You don't have to follow me, I'll meet you here.'

He used the time she was away to count the trees and look at the small waves breaking. She came back and touched him lightly on the shoulder.

'You didn't say if you wanted red or white,' she said, 'so I got red. They wouldn't open it in the shop for me. Bastards.'

She hacked the plastic off with a key that she used to press in the cork. There was a crystal attached to the keyring.

She drank some of the wine and pulled that face again. He drank more than his fair share, as she pointed out.

'What brings you here?'

'My mother, in her womb,' she said. 'I am a local too. *Muy loca*, you could say. My mother used to.'

'Used to?'

'Yes. She doesn't say it now.'

She told him that her mother was Spanish, but that her dark looks came from her father.

'Who was not Spanish,' she added, after another gulp of wine. 'Do you like the wine?'

'Yes.'

'A bit oaky, perhaps.'

'You know a lot about wine?' he asked.

'You mean, do I drink a lot? No, but my father did. He drank to excess, and beyond that. Here's to Daddy,' she said, and tapped the bottle against his boot. 'Does your da drink?'

'He's dead,' he said.

'Not from drink?'

'No, an accident.'

'My dad died of drink. It was a sort of accident too ... And what brings *you* here?'

'I don't know. My girlfriend was going somewhere with her friends, so I came here. Got on a bus. Actually,' he said, realizing it as he spoke, 'I don't know where this is.'

She laughed so much that she had to lie flat on the grass. He didn't know the name of the place, and he didn't know her name either. She was very attractive, lying there, and he had to look away.

'I suppose you were going to walk down to the sea,' she said after a while, once she had stopped shaking. 'I'll take you there, if you like.'

They walked, with the wine bottle still being passed between them, though it was almost empty now. She was Veronica, but he was to call her Vee, since her name was embarrassing. He didn't see why.

'You know someone else called Veronica?'

'I have to admit ...'

They passed the sand dunes and came to a spot where there were two paths and a signpost. He hung back and let Vee choose the path. There was some silence between them that wasn't oppressive and he lapsed into a dreamy state. A thick barrier of thorn-trees seemed to prevent them going on, but Vee knew a way through.

'What is your girlfriend like?' she asked. It came out of the blue, but he somehow expected it. He didn't know how to answer: his instinct was to play down her importance to him, which would be transparent to Vee. Why was he thinking like this? Vee had no interest in him, it was clear.

'She has red hair,' he said. 'She's livelier than me.'

'Not as adventurous.'

'What makes you say that?'

'You are here, aren't you?'

'She's more adventurous than me, she's livelier, and she has red hair.'

'How long have you been together?'

'That's not easy,' he said, truthfully. 'There were two phases.'

'Who broke it off before?'

'I did.'

'She'll break it off next,' she said. It didn't seem malicious, only precise.

He found himself speaking, brokenly at first, but eventually freely. 'I think I made a mistake with her,' he said. 'Last week. We were walking along the road and this old couple passed us holding hands and I said something about us being like that some day. It was just that at that moment it felt impossible that we would ever separate. I felt her hand shrinking, if you can imagine that.'

She squeezed his hand then and said, 'Yes, I can imagine that,' and started to speak about herself. She had been engaged recently, to an older man who was moving to a job in Australia. He moved earlier than expected, and without her. 'What makes me angry,' she said, 'isn't that he left me. It's the idea that I was engaged. How could I do that to myself?'

There was a man and a young boy on the beach, a father and son it looked like, and the father was showing the boy how to fly a kite. It looked awkward for some reason.

'His dad's right-handed,' Vee said, 'but he's left-handed.'

'I don't think I would ever have seen that,' he said.

'I'm sharp-witted,' she said. 'My mother used to say that. She died when I was eight.'

The boy had given up and run into the water and

now the man was carrying him out, 'like an exhibit in a museum,' Vee said. They laughed at the boy's screams.

The sun was very bright on the white sand and it made the blue water white also, at times. They had stepped back from the water and were looking out over the scene, with their backs to the trees and the village.

'My dad was an alcoholic,' she said, 'and he was a gambler. Jesus, my life is an old blues song. My mum would throw his cards out of the house but not his drink. I found him with an old crony of his one night and they were gambling using Tarot cards. That's beautiful. He didn't die with us – he went to die in Zennor, in Cornwall. You'd like it there.' She said it as if she knew him, and he asked 'Why?', hoping she would prove it.

'Oh, I don't know,' she said. 'I like it. In the church there's a wood carving of a mermaid. Things like that ... This wine's finished,' she said, her mood changing, 'and I'm not drunk yet. If you weren't such a baby I'd buy more. Oh, look, I didn't mean it.'

He wasn't as unhappy as his face showed, especially when she left his side and stood in an intriguing pose. It was a prelude to her doing cartwheels on the sand. He was happy just to watch her.

Somebody out of sight of them was shouting 'Adam!' in a desperate voice. Vee stopped and shaded her eyes. The man appeared at the crest of a sand dune – it was the father of the boy with the kite: his son, Adam, must be missing. Vee skipped up to him.

The boy had run off when his father was in the phone box, except that it wasn't his father, it was a priest, and the boy lived in the residential school nearby: he had a history of running off. He was epileptic and he hallucinated a black dog that chased him. Once, when he lived in England, he was rescued as he was running at a cliff-edge in Beachy Head. The priest was distraught. He told Vee all this.

She walked back over to her drinking friend and repeated the story, telling him to stay here. He disliked the man when he heard he was a priest. Vee had an idea where the boy might be.

Less than ten minutes later she was holding a docile Adam by the hand. The priest, who had gone back to the phone-box, and then come back to stand awkwardly on the sand, rushed up to them.

'There's a place just along the beach that we used to call the Cave. I've hidden there before,' she told him when they were alone again. 'I used to be in that school too, for a while.' They were on the path now going into the village, probably to say goodbye. Vee stopped at an old newspaper that was stuck to the ground. Her head was tilted and she was reading something.

'That's our childhoods,' she said, 'yours and mine.' He looked and saw an article on the Moors murders, and the photographs of two of the children.

'I didn't say anything about my childhood,' he said.

'Didn't you? ... Have it your way.' She came out of her trance and smiled again.

'Do you possess any brothers?' she asked. She asked it in Spanish and he answered in Spanish, but he said *cuatro* instead of *tres*, a mistake that amused her when he told her all his brothers' names. She wanted to know what Robert was like: he was her age.

'That was unfair,' she said, after he'd tried a few words. 'Nobody likes describing their brother. Look, I've got something for you.'

She put her hand into his inside coat pocket and took out the book of Lorca's poems that he carried everywhere; then she picked a flower from the grass and pressed it into the book.

'How did you know the book was there?'

'I've gone through all your pockets,' she said. 'I told you I'd been to that school.'

They came to a blue bus shelter that was set back into some dark rock which rose steeply from the side of the road. It was best, he thought, if she left him now, but he didn't want her to go. She didn't want to go. That changed when a woman came along and stood next to them despite there being so much room. Vee's face turned a different colour. She didn't have to tell him that the woman was a local.

The hostility was not only on Vee's part, and the woman, who was holding a tartan vanity case, looked out of the corner of her eye at them. He went to move away but Vee held his arm. They whispered very dramatically, hands cupped from mouths to ears. He had the feeling he would never see her again. He looked at her and memorized the details: the long blue dress – it hadn't embarrassed her when it fell back over her as she did the cartwheels – and her frost-blue eyes, the eyes of an insomniac, he thought later. Her hair was black – Spanish-Irish, she had told him (did that mean that her father was Irish?). Her skin was pale. There was a friendship bracelet.

From the seat on the left side of the bus he didn't see her properly to wave goodbye, but it gave him a good view of the gnarled trees on that side of the road. His mouth was dry, because of the wine, but also from fear. He didn't understand it. He felt it strongly later that night when he wrote what seemed a million words – they streamed out of him, with no effort on his part except to try to understand what he was saying. So much of what happened in the day with Vee went into it, but not everything, and there were other things that came from nowhere. He didn't put in, for instance, the very last thing she did as the bus approached.

He was taking money out of his pocket for the fare when he remembered that he'd promised to pay for half the wine. He pushed some money into Vee's hands, but she rejected it. She said, not even coyly, 'I'm not a prostitute ... Unluckily for you.' Then she stood in front of the woman and stared at her and said, 'There is no Buddha-nature in you.' He smiled a very wide smile, whereas she was stony-faced. She said as she passed him, 'That should keep them interested.'

Retro

1

The bedroom – feels like a hotel room now. I suppose I would be abroad somewhere. From the window I can expect to see palm trees, the passing couples to be more affectionate, but only the noise of the city doesn't let me down. There's been so much demolition in these streets that sounds float in the air; sound foreign. And this – the tiny plane she made from a nightclub card ... really floats.

What does she think I'll do? Exit through this fourth-floor window? Her stupid friend said 'This would be a good place to jump from,' and by rights I should have pushed her out (the friend) there and then. I could have cheated fate. There's the word 'cheated' again. It's beautiful of her to leave a note, and to tell me she never cheated on me, 'not till now, and not now either'. It was our trial reunion and it's over. The note explains.

Yesterday's clothes are all right, I couldn't smell her in them if I tried. Her glass and her plate, hardly touched, are still there. I'll clear it all away; first I want to read again. There's an inconsistency in the loops of the js, but there are only a few, all except one in the word 'just': 'it's just that' – she's overfond of the phrase. That's the biggest flaw, the fact that she put her name to it. Lovers shouldn't sign their farewells. Though it's true she wouldn't regard herself as a lover now ...

I don't care about the loops of her js.

It's not a lie to say that I never mistook her for my mother – or my mother for her, whatever the grammar is. And yet since I read the note and slept again, slept all morning, it's my mother I've dreamt about: dreams of separation, but so beautiful I wish I could go on dreaming them. There was a Hopper-type landscape: sprawling low white mansion, a vast serene lawn, with glistening road winding away from view, and me there – a younger self, I'd say, and my mother from thirty years ago. Sky a deep, deep blue. Then lightning cracks over the whole landscape, coming to rest between our hands (not to *rest*); between left hand and right hand, so that we can't touch.

I was sixteen the first time this happened – dumped for a musician, in the days before I became one myself. Then nothing in my twenties. Contentment for months at a time until I moved on, they never seemed to mind. Meeting Joan was like – well, I've thought this one out before. As if the gypsy woman in that awful kitsch painting from my childhood stepped out of the frame to say hello. I loved that gypsy. Joan admitted later it was a bolt from the blue for her also (my dream again), but you wouldn't have known. That's why I liked to tease her when I found out she had a name, Karen, that she never used. K. J. My beautiful cagey darling, I said more than twice.

So nothing prepared me for the Big Scene; and after the Big Scene, for the months of disintegration until she called again. She didn't call; it was another note. What I remember best about those months was the supermarket. The basket got weighed down – even though I was making less money, almost none since the band stopped touring – with whatever passes in those stores for exotic; blood oranges even. And most of it rotted.

I didn't expect it, but I'm not surprised. Maybe this second time around she's been toying with me. I noticed how she wanted to pay for everything, and because it didn't matter I let her. We went to see a film about a man and a woman who loved their pets. There was nothing to talk about afterwards and the end had begun.

Now, speaking to strangers the way my father did, when he stood in his shirt in all weathers with a rolled up newspaper in his hand, rubbing his forehead, I am disengaging myself from that alias she rejected, but not because I've wanted her back. The man unlocking the door of the fish truck didn't respond when I told him I'd fed a filleting machine once, during the herring season twelve years ago. And why should he respond? Because I have seen men talking like that all through my life. They go out for their milk and paper, or put a rose on their wife's bosom instead. I walk by, silent, discerning. And with Joan at my side, my eyes brimful of contempt, I'd have a smile they could never fathom ... But he bolted the door shut, so that I saw the fish factory's whole logo, and sighed with an *intake* of breath, while I (how stupidly?) waved him away.

Geoff will miss me. He'd only just got used to seeing me again; I noticed last week he stopped looking at Joan whenever I asked him anything. I watched him grow from a baby (six months) to a boy who'll start school in August. He's the only child I've seen develop. He looked so good in the little sailor's outfit. He was two then.

Perhaps I changed because we became so close, the three of us cooped up in that little flat. I convinced myself: too much closeness stifles me. I see only bright reds and yellows when I think of that time, the colours of the toy bricks I'd build up for Geoff to punch down. Why can I only be happy in retrospect? But I wasn't happy. I was hungry.

I was going alone to the gigs, and coming back alone, and I didn't sleep around in between, but I was looking at women. The numbers we did started to mean something. I always felt sort of looked up to: I was smart, everyone knew, but I shifted from foot to foot and mumbled responses, weighing what I said. Somebody called me Shane when I came out with 'A guitar is only a tool,' and the name was used after that any time I said something enigmatic or stood in a doorway. It was a joke, but I started to live it.

I wanted to become the music, if that means anything. To be a *thing* from which nothing but otherness flowed. In the end I couldn't see a way to make it happen other than to take a sullen brunette back with me, make love to her on the living room floor and present her to Joan at breakfast. Only, it was Geoff who discovered her first. This was something returned to by Joan again and again, in the scene that followed.

I could have scripted the brunette's part: 'I'm out of here,' she did literally say, making a movement with her hands as if she was brushing off dirt. I had to stop her leaving with Joan's lucky throw. Joan just kept saying 'What? What?' up close to my face, which disconcerted me: I would have been happier at a distance, looking at her out of the corner of my eye. The breakfast we'd just begun – and I mean the bowls, cups, plates – got quickly scattered and thrown. I was trying to communicate the incommunicable point of view of the alias I now was, but he was too slow-moving, too profound an entity to cope with the frantic blur of Joan. There was something she was holding above her head that must have had value for me, which she was threatening to smash – so my glance up at her revealed. Then I looked and saw the kitchen knife pressed against her raised arm. Then I heard what she was saying. 'Is this it? This what you want?' And laughter. 'Because I'm going to disappoint you, sweetheart.' She wanted me out. I had to bow to her spirit's supremacy at this moment. There was no point leaning against a door, making a gnomic utterance now.

I'd brought a woman back whose nakedness at the breakfast bar had startled Joan's pyjama'd son into loud tears, then Joan herself had entered naked. I was the only fully clothed person at the scene. I wonder if she thinks of that. I don't want to be by myself recreating it all.

As if it matters. What's important now is not to fall. Because she won't be back, there's no hope: that's the good news. She can indulge her friend on long nights drinking rosé and listen to monologues on how hateful I am. It worked before, up to a point. After a while she stopped listening and wanted me again. It's what I can't work out. Friends said she needed a father for Geoff, but I was never very good at that ... even though she insisted I was. After sex once. Not how good a lover I was; how good a father to her son. It sounds less, I suppose, until it's said to you, then you know it's more.

'Joan's gone, man, she's gone,' I can hear Rafael say

already. And: 'Move on.'

2

'Wanted, haunted,' Jim sang, higher this time, as if the pressure inside him were mounting (his conquest from Montreal, an intelligent blonde waitress who wore red leather, had five weeks ago packed her things into his best suitcase and left), while everybody else groaned or writhed some more. Rafael, who had leapt to his defence previously – he'd said, 'We could squeeze one or two with words into the set, though *not those words*' – slumped in his chair and pulled Therese's hat over his face. Therese was out of the room with Billy.

'The place is definitely *not* haunted,' Joan said, half to Dub alone, her head in the crook of his arm. 'That fat bastard owner's just a greedy farmer.'

'Steady,' Dub said, releasing a fold of flab from his belt. Joan ignored the laughter in the room, saying: 'But we paid top dollar.' Somehow this was even funnier ...

They'd placed an ad in two music papers. They were thinking of something along the lines of Aleister Crowley's old home on the shores of Loch Ness, somewhere atmospheric to work the new set into shape. Jim had covered the backs and fronts and insides of envelopes with bad lyrics for months. A joke to the rest of them – like everything else – Jim took it achingly seriously. He was getting thinner.

'George heard the kitchen door slam when nobody was about,' Rafael offered. 'Isn't that true?'

'Yes,' George said, speaking into his knees.

'When was this?' Joan asked.

'Yesterday.'

'A mysterious door slam is not enough. Ow.' Dub was drumming on her thigh, saying 'I'm hungry again, Joan, baby,' and 'When's Don Juan coming back? Took him a long time to get over Mink.' Dub was the sarcasm king in the band.

'Enough chauvinist bullshit. Rafael, hold this.' Rafael accepted the wine, and Joan, unhappy, uncurled, stood up and walked to the blacked-out window. It was an hour later, when the others had left for the hotel bar, that she took one of the ornamental oil lamps and tracked Billy down. He was there in the attic room, but not Therese.

'I think to shower, or for something ...' Billy turned over and put his face into the pillow. One disarrayed sheet of the bedclothes was all that covered him, but even this Joan drew back.

'They were making fun of you downstairs, and I felt sorry for you,' she said, curling into him, tracing slow esses on his back while he shuddered and took her arm, holding it round him, to stop her.

'Therese won't like me being here,' she said. 'Do you love her?'

'She's Therese.'

'You're one cold fish.'

'Cold son of a bitch,' he said and began kissing her. After a while he got up and sat in the chair next to the bed. Joan moved so that her head was at the foot of the bed. It meant that one of her breasts became exposed.

'Don't sit there looking at me, thinking about her.'

'You're making this up. And what about Dub?'

'Oh, Dub,' she said, with a playful indifference that delighted him. 'I've only known him five minutes. Known you six,' she said, trailing her voice off, making the 'six' sound like 'sex'.

They looked quickly round to see Therese walk in. She was holding one towel and wearing another; looked at her, then him, and finally left with a hand in the air, as if to say: 'Whatever.'

Billy stood up, rubbed his forehead and sat back down, answering 'No' to Joan's question should she go after her. They didn't speak again for a while, and Joan, like an amused schoolgirl in class, was having a hard time suppressing her laughter.

'What?'

'Nothing. It's just that, well, you've a reputation for not holding onto women, but this must be bad even by your standards. I mean, if it's the end.'

'That's what you wanted.'

Joan moved uncomfortably onto an elbow and regarded him.

'I'm supposed to say "No, it's not" to that. Are you angry?'

'To tell you the truth ... '

'Don't say that. It means you're about to lie.'

'To tell you the truth, I'm more hungry than angry, and I'm thinking of nipping down to the kitchen, but if Therese ... '

'There's no food in the house anywhere,' she said, not calmly enough for her liking. 'So don't go.'

He smiled at that, and got into bed, pressing his cold flesh against her side so that she squealed – and went on squealing, the thought that Therese might hear silencing her intermittently. Eventually they locked together, cold flesh or not, and neither of them smiled, though both were happy. They couldn't bear to look each other in the eye.

'I wanted this to happen,' was all that he said at first, and Joan, who needed to hear more, understood that she wouldn't have to prompt him. Nonetheless she drew a finger along his spine.

'But I had no idea ... ' he said, taking hold of her hand, bringing it to his crotch. 'You arrived with Dub and I thought "That's that".' She felt his guilt at the mention of Dub's name, and attempted to stroke it away, but he wanted to know more about them.

'Why don't you tell me about Mink first?' she asked.

'Mink?'

'That's who you went out with last, right?'

'They call Monica "Mink"? I had no idea,' he said,

laughing as though the boys in the band were with them in the room. Joan would have to be the one to speak.

'We met at a swing park in the Meadows. A beautiful summer's day. Well, actually, I'd seen him the time I first saw you, playing the Venue, but I never really noticed him. You don't remember but I spoke to you that night. I was with a friend. She remembers you – you turned your back on her.'

'I was probably stoned.'

'He was with his wee boy Karl, when I met him, and they seemed *so* sweet together.'

'You play on the swings a lot?'

'No,' she said, and grew quiet. Then, to break the spell of moroseness, she teased him about Monica again.

'Think of a cross between Lizzie Borden and Sylvia Plath. And be glad it was Therese who walked in on us, not her.'

'I don't understand that,' she said, 'but I suppose I do. Who are those other girls you mentioned?' When he started to explain she laughed at him, dug her thumbs into his armpits and raised herself so that they were face to face.

'You really do think I'm thick. Think I'm another groupie?' She pressed hard with her thumbs until he squirmed free, then pounded him softly with her fists, stopping when she heard a door bang somewhere. Then there was the gravel of the driveway, Therese's footsteps leading away from the house. Billy seemed to let a pocket of air finally escape from his chest.

'I feel sad for her,' Joan said quietly. It was the last mention of Therese.

He flipped her onto her front and lay on top, managing to keep some of his weight from pressing on her, and just about able to see that she was still smiling. He didn't feel like telling her his life's story, and when she turned back round to him, and it felt as though neither were initiating it, they made love: they had known they would. He was conscious of still smelling of Therese.

Afterwards they dressed, fully, and the possibility

of going outside was there. Billy found a heel of bread to toast, and Joan made tea for them both in a comically large mug, sprinkling the powdered milk into it with love. There was a huge wine-red sheet hanging over the pulley and dividing the kitchen in two, and they sat one side of it feeling protected, warming their hands on the blue glaze of the mug. Billy picked up a guitar and improvised a tune to one of the envelope-lyrics propped against the bread-board; Joan didn't laugh but asked him to play something else instead. He obliged with a Spanish-American song he guiltily knew to be effective, Joan making him translate and then correcting him. *You are tall and slender, just like your mother, sparkling brunette, just like your mother. Blessed be the branch that from the trunk is born* ... He was in fact pleased that the song's seductiveness failed. He looked at Joan's face and staring back at him was the gypsy woman from that awful painting from years ago. He had never recalled it before.

She was asking him a question.

Yes, yes, he was still hungry. No, the others wouldn't think to shop, they were all drunk by now.

They put on coats and Joan put on a scarf and gloves, for the mile walk to the delicatessen.

'Will I make a list?' he asked, his childlike uncertainty more than pleasing her. She looked round them.

'If you can make one with lipstick and Rizla papers, yes.'

Arid

Before, I was like a baby whose every encounter is with the new. Then I thought that perhaps I was unable to feel this way again – as if my mind were breaking into leaf – and put off making any fresh journeys. It is too easy to call it escape – climbing into the car and letting myself be driven through new landscapes, where all moons are new moons, and I might learn to live somehow differently.

We still can't decide which year it was, 91 or 92, when we remind ourselves of each detail again, at my prompting, over some bottles of Retsina, say. We went there, he says, six months after the Temple Monster's death; I say it was another year after that. Never having met my friend the Temple Monster, in our semi-drunken evenings he will still, to placate me, adopt my internal calendar for his use.

Which is fine by me.

I held the road atlas in my hands, looked at the place we were going to, and traced a finger along the route, asking him to repeat it slowly, because alongside my thirst for the new was a desire to imagine everything beforehand. I was finding it hard keeping the geography of it all in mind, and left to navigate alone he strayed into the one major town between his home and there. The dead-ends and panic-stops and turning back on ourselves only amused me. Then we moved into real countryside. I had always loved roads like these, roads flanked by primitive-looking telegraph poles – Dalí-crutches, a friend of mine called them. I stayed happy and relaxed even as the journey threatened to become a frustrating dream: the owner of the villa we'd rented couldn't be found, and we had to wait, an hour almost, parked outside her granite house in the afternoon sunshine. She arrived to squint half-quizzically at us through the windscreen, a breezy woman golfer I decided, and disappeared into the granite. I sat on in the car.

'If I give you money ...' he said, and stopped at that,

and I stared, not understanding, at the neatly folded tenner he pointed towards me. When he said I could maybe get some food I knew that he wanted to look over the place by himself, to own it for a few minutes. I strolled to where the shops were.

The shopkeeper in the first shop frowned at me, and I wondered about the intensity of my look. He mentioned the weather. 'Good for October,' he said.

'Amazing for October,' I said, rescuing my good mood. The word 'amazing' marked me out as a tourist.

Outside, I smoked one cigarette and then another, looking across to the sea (there was a thin chiming sound in the air) when I saw him walking, half-skipping along the street, his face a satisfied smile.

'How's the place?'

'Fine. I'll tell you about it,' he said, eyeing up the exterior of the hotel opposite – a McEwan's Export sign hung above the door – 'inside'.

The bar was too small to sit comfortably at, and we carried the drinks to a window table, table number seven in fact: I drew a line with my finger through the seven. There was a heavy smell of old cooked meat.

'Thanks for inviting us here,' I said.

'What do you mean "thanks"?'

I wasn't genuinely feeling meek. He had built up too much time at work and he wanted company.

'Do you know when she'll be here yet?' he asked.

'Tomorrow noon, I think. I'll phone later.'

'There's a phone in one of the bedrooms,' he said.

'That's right – what's the place like?'

'It's a nice place.'

I felt the beer affecting my head already, and imagined the cerebral neurones clacking together like dominoes: it wasn't long since I'd left work at the Epileptic Colony.

'This is my first holiday since Greece,' I said.

'You were in Greece?'

'Yes,' I said, suddenly angry. 'I showed you the photographs.'

'Greece was where I slept with the whale,' he said.

'Yes, I remember that ... You shouldn't refer to her as a whale.'

'Let me, I'm on holiday.'

It had always been after two drinks that we found we must stay and see the evening out, since university days, but this time we left after the second drink. If the beer hadn't made us hungry, we would have gone on to explore the harbour then. But we were hungry and there were hours of daylight left.

The villa, Blue Heaven, had sky-blue roof tiles and was in a cluster of white buildings. It was an awkward, backward-L-shape, with five steps up to it and a green watering can at the door. It was called Blue Heaven but it had a street number as well, which I found odd.

'That woman must have children, maybe grandchildren now,' I remember thinking as we steered ourselves through the hall, past handlebars like rams' horns. He pulled back a sliding screen and exposed the toilet and curtainless stone-floored shower and I said: 'That's unusual ... What's behind that door?' Behind the next door was the bedroom we wouldn't use.

'It's definitely damp.'

He was keen to close the door on it and move us up a flight of stairs to the habitable part, to show that he hadn't wasted his money.

I stretched out on the long brown sofa at the top of the stairs, waving him towards the plush kitchen like a servant. Neither of us had the patience to cook anything elaborate just yet. I pointed out the seat in the corner, identical to one in the flat we used to share, with its speckled green and red covering.

'Somebody's even nailed the leather straps down like you did,' he said, inspecting it.

There was a bowl of glass fruit on the table and

then the room's best feature, a long, almost wall-length window that faced the beach.

'I'd like to go running on that,' I said. 'I'm going to go running tomorrow.'

'When are you phoning?'

'Not before tonight. Relax.'

We read the meter and checked that everything worked. We were both silently calculating how long a walk to see the sights would use up before we uncovered the next bar.

'Let's just go now,' I said, switching the kettle off.

'All right.'

The sky still wasn't dark. I managed to turn the wrong corner and walk into the small maze of white houses.

'Only you could get lost in a place like this,' he said. 'You weren't always like that.'

'I used to try to hold everything in my mind, I actually worked at it,' I said.

'I've been having amazing dreams lately. When I've had time off and go back to sleep after I wake up. About ten o' clock, eleven o' clock. Even if they're nightmares I want to fall asleep again and go back into them.'

Now I knew what the chiming sound had been as we came to the long stone jetty and saw the boats congregated there, rocking in the choppy water. Ahead of us was a huge bleak building like a granary. We could see from a distance that its windows were broken.

He'd had a dream this morning. There was a detail I latched on to, about him walking along a promenade. As a young couple walk past him pushing a pram, the woman deliberately hits a wheel against his ankle.

'You're limping!' I said.

'My foot's been agony all day.'

It was his fear of being outnumbered on the holiday. He had booked it and paid for it and should be calling the shots, but together we intimidated him. We were the fertile couple (he had moved away from the water to let us past) and he was the arid solitary. I said all this brutally, but in an analytical voice, a critic's, and watched to see how he reacted.

'Maybe,' he said. 'But that really did happen. When I had my ankle in plaster. I was in Portobello and I saw this bitch woman workmate of Janine's coming towards me with her boyfriend. I was embarrassed because I knew she'd said Janine should dump *me*, not her husband. It wasn't that bit I didn't understand.'

I had begun to notice the bright green water lapping against the wall below me; watching it, I felt hypnotized.

'Remember *Vertigo*, when Kim Novak falls into San Francisco Bay?' I said. 'That close-up of the water. I love that scene.'

We continued to the bleak building and climbed up to one of its giant empty windows and looked in – on some lobster pots, I remember. Night was coming on. I was enjoying the moment, shivering a little, saying, 'Listen to the boats.' Then we doubled back to the Harbour Inn.

It was still early and there were only a few inside, lined up at the bar. The table we sat at, near the front, was solid oak, which we appreciated, and I think we both felt freer, as if we ourselves were salty old seadogs. A woman our age walked in with a black dog and said to a leather-jacketed man, 'I dreamt about you last night.' We tried to hide our smiles and I said quietly: 'Everybody's dreaming.'

'It's the sea air.'

Instead of being embarrassed by her candour, the man smiled down at her and asked for details as he bought her a drink. It struck me that they had lived here and known each other all their lives. They had probably slept together half a dozen times when they were seventeen, and very occasionally, if they were lonely enough, they still did. That was written in their eyes – not exactly twinkling – as they smuggled messages to one another through their talk, messages that, if I'm honest, didn't reach me.

'Or you could risk sleeping in the bunkbeds downstairs ... '

I smiled deafly to encourage him, but it seemed he was finished. We would stay another two, three hours, smoking and talking, mostly about Janine, though in the past tense.

'I'll phone now,' I said, setting more drinks down. 'But not here.'

'I'm sure I saw a phone box.'

'I remember where it is.'

'I'll come with you,' he said, half getting up then looking at the drinks he'd nudged. 'Or maybe not.'

The smell of the sea took me by surprise for a moment. The phone box was close to the awkward shop.

'It's me.'

'Hello.'

'Hello?'

'Where are you?'

'In a phone box. I said I'd phone.'

'I've waited in.'

'That's good.'

'Is it? ... How's the place?'

'Blue heaven.'

'Are you alone?'

'In the phone-box, yes. Listen, when are you coming?'

'You know the answer to that. Tomorrow, twelve, half twelve. You're going to wait for me in Kirkcaldy bus station. Do you know the way yet?'

'We strayed into there today.'

'That's good.'

'I've been drinking.'

'I know. What's the house like?'

'Blue heaven.'

'Stop saying that.'

'It's a nice place. We've got a double bed.'

I was breathing heavily, she said. It only made me

want to speak in a seductive voice, until I couldn't think what else to say.

'That's right,' she said when I dried up. 'Anything slow or dark. You love it.'

I talked about the bar.

'It's a salty place. This girl walked in and said to one old boy, "I dreamt about you last night." Not so old, maybe.'

'I dreamt about you.'

'Really? What?'

The silence wasn't comfortable.

I said something then, but my voice, I'm sure, sounded tinny.

'Did you get morose tonight?' she asked eventually.

'How do you mean?'

'Thinking about Martin.'

'Morose is unfair.'

'Did you?'

'No I didn't. I wasn't thinking about him.'

'.........'

'.........'

'I better go.'

'No, don't.'

I asked her what work had been like and where she would be standing tomorrow. I was listening for warmth to re-enter her voice, but I couldn't think of the right thing. There had always been the one right thing that I managed to stumble upon and say, like the poem I wrote at the start, in the Colony, when the girl in the room below joked about the noise we made at night. 'What men think of me, and women of you,' it had begun, and ended 'Whatever men think of me, and women of you.' Or pointing out the squirrels outside her window.

'I *have* to go,' she said finally, and I countered with 'Twelve, half twelve,' equally briskly.

'Twelve, make it,' she said, and the phone clicked.

The walk back round to the Harbour Inn didn't seem longer or the night any emptier, and I was struck by how well I was taking things, but what things? It seemed senseless to dig trouble out from the back of my mind. The sea, the harbour wall, the black rectangle of the 'granary', and that chiming sound of boats again ... were so much more real than thought.

At least the pub was warm. In his eyes I could see that he had deteriorated in the time I was away. The couple had gone, or else shifted to one of the booths at the back, and three men were playing dominoes with white dominoes. Nothing was going to happen.

The next thing was the fluorescent strip-light in the kitchen-alcove. I was wondering about it, waiting to be handed supper. There was a film on in the corner of the room that gradually drew us in, *A Farewell to Arms* I think it was. A woman was lying in a hospital bed and a man was speaking to her.

I had a feeling of infinity. Drifting in and out of sleep had dismantled the film's plot, but it was in the film too, perhaps, that feeling. I broke out of my trance at some point to go downstairs, where I decided to shave – shaving at night drunk was a speciality of mine (I always managed to produce some blood).

The sheets of the bed were turned down a little, which I hadn't noticed before. Whatever came on after the film he was watching alone now. I'd said goodnight. I decided that it wasn't worthwhile to go to bed naked. There was the phone. It was so old, like the one we had when I was young – mustard yellow, with a round dial. The television would cover the sound of dialling. I picked up the phone, but I could think of just two numbers, the Temple Monster's and my own, which was also hers.

I'd been lying in the dark a long time when he passed the door and said goodnight again. I was imagining the dream he'd told me, in the hope that it would drag me to sleep. Scene succeeded scene until somehow the promenade woman was stretched out naked on a chequered-marble floor, crawling backwards on her elbows with her head thrown back.

After a while, possibly hours, the images faded and I got out of bed. It was brighter in the main room with the window showing the sea. I stood there watching out, very deliberately not thinking. I had neglected to do something and it troubled me. I had let him close the door on the downstairs room too quickly. So I picked my way through the darkness and down the stairs and was standing at the door.

The light worked and I looked round just as before: the same damp smell, but how white everything was! The beds were so white because the white duvets were coverless. I heard a drip and then saw something land on the top bunk. Immediately I went over and felt that the duvet was wet. I pulled it back from the mattress and stood back.

They had something inside them like the inside of a marble. There were three that I saw, huge, cricket-like insects, almost transparent ...

Sam and Step

My stepsister was a foot in front of me on the ice, cursing the steep slope that would bring us to the farm and the square building that was my home now. Her husband, who had been like a brother to me once before, was rat-tat-tatting a beach branch he'd picked up and making ice-holes. No two people could have looked less like each other, I imagined, than they did then, and of course I sided with the childlike Sam. Step's fairytale wickedness was a legend. I didn't believe in it, the excuses for it.

'Where is this palace?' she was singing at me. You knew when her voice became sing-song she was really at the edge. I was already carrying most of the things, and slipping more than anybody.

'Through the archway there,' I said.

Sam was doing something, taking the childlike thing too far, so that Step snapped and my blue raku vase was gone. I should have given her books to carry.

She was soon upsetting the cats, moving furniture and sending Sam into dark corners. I liked to stand back in these situations and watch her bad eye. She disapproved of much, but appreciated the sketch of her, done on the first day we were alone together, I'd left lying out with some other work.

Back then, when I was at art school, her father had got a flat for me. We found – I mean myself and Sam, who hadn't met her then, wouldn't for a while yet – a blood stain under the bed. The previous tenant was a schizophrenic and had pinned Barbie dolls above the bed in diamond shapes with rusty hatpins. I visualize smaller dolls than Barbies, if that matters. Somebody who knew let us know.

I made the sketch to save having to speak to her much, I suppose. It was a dismal afternoon. One strap of her top had fallen from her shoulder. 'Remind me how I am related to you again,' I said. It was apropos of nothing and she produced one of her rare smiles.

Now Sam was testing the springiness of the bed and discovering that it was like a door. Step took a twenty-pound note from her wallet, gave me it, and walked briskly across the room, almost taking Sam by the hand as she left. I wondered guiltily if I had put the sketch on the little canvas stool on purpose to increase her generosity, which isn't the word. She was a daunting benefactress.

The next time I saw Sam he had a baseball cap on sideways and a few kids round him laughing. That was at the lock-ups, where he kept his old Citroën. It was my old street, Step having moved into my father's house. I went back there to take photographs of the area – I had recorded the changes over the past decade, which were not too numerous in fact – and clippings of the weeds in the garden, foxgloves mainly. The old tree was formidable and kept half the garden in shade. Sam said hello but didn't stop tormenting one kid by holding his skull at arm's length and bouncing a football while the kid scooped at empty air.

'Come for more flowers?'

'Flowers and photographs.'

'She's out, if you're wanting to know,' he said glancing up.

'Not specially.' He knew my visits were timed to avoid her. In seven years, since mum married and moved out, I hadn't once been in the house. Dad had died three years before that.

'I'll be out here, if you're coming back this way,' he said. I grunted to reassure him.

'See you, Sam.'

I looked along the familiar street. My mouth wanted to speak a word, something intimate, a name which the street conjured. I actually did say 'Ligeia,' from the Edgar Allan Poe story, but that wasn't right. I appreciated the different colours of doors and different windows, not like the uniformity that used to prevail. The lock-ups were the same, though. One night I convinced myself I had seen a photograph of Hitler in a room above one lock-up: an old hand was shifting it along a mantelpiece when it tilted towards me. This was proof that the dead, the fascist dead, populated these suburbs, which I believed at sixteen. Now there was a new crop of children and my old friend Sam among them, and Step. The children weren't their children, which I would have liked to have asked about.

On a low wall outside one house was something new to photograph – fresh graffiti, chalked there: MALKY SPADE KING. I smiled and turned, half-affectionate, for the first time that day to face our old house.

It wasn't quite right. I saw through the viewfinder that the front door was open. Careless, I thought. The door was blowing in and out with the breeze, not violently enough to close over. I let myself believe that it was a signal, summoning me, like the ice cream van summoning children outside.

There had never been a gate to hesitate at. I hardly needed to push the door wider to get inside: so many years on, and the same smell, encountered nowhere else. I used to think it was shut windows and the same cooking week after week. Step would have tried to get rid of it, but even she would be used to it now, exasperated but not by the fact that the house wouldn't take on her smell. Within seconds I was walking up the fourteen stairs to the top landing. Everything was flowery, bright – the stairs' carpet, the wallpaper – but I looked and saw that it wasn't excessively, it was just a feeling, a feeling that I'd stepped inside a painting by Marc Chagall. I should have done this before, I thought. Clearly I had been missing out these seven years.

When I walked outside again the sun had gone. I knew that I should tell Sam about the door. Walking in the direction of the lock-ups and making adjustments to the camera, I realized that I hadn't taken any photographs of inside, which was decent of me, I suppose; well-mannered. Besides, remembering the Chagall feeling, I was sure I'd be back.

Round at the lock-ups, it seemed that I had missed

Sam, and I was standing wondering where next to go when I saw him in a car, not the Citroën, a new car. There was a head beside him; I recognized the tormented boy of earlier. I felt shy about reappearing like this. Leaning on the roof from the back of the car and looking in, I quickly looked away again. The two were holding hands. No, the boy's hand was wrapped up in Sam's, as though they were playing Paper, Scisssors, Stone and Sam was winning. That occurs to me now. The thing I noticed at the time was how round their hands were together, like one round plump hand or a large peach, coming apart when I made my presence known. That was with a knock on the roof. Sam looked at me, the car door opened, I mentioned the open house door, turned and, guilty-innocent, walked away. I kept on walking, away from our street, imagining at one point that I'd heard him say 'Thanks.'

The outside world was gone. What I saw was the obscene plump hand and then other hands, beckoning me back to the image that wanted to obsess me – her hands, the ones I struggled with that December afternoon. They were long, as thin as ever; there was a ring on her wedding-ring finger that I didn't ask about. The rain kept up outside and the gas fire pretended to be effective. She had taken off a long black coat with enormous buttons, had a rubber band in her hair, and was looking directly into my eyes. That only mattered when I was working on her face. I didn't know it, or I knew it, but not fully – that here she was on a plate. I considered it noble to reject anything offered to me like this – hated accepting the flat from her father – but Sam was greedier. That's a lie. I was greedy, the greediest of us all, but my horizons were limited.

I walked and took photographs of myself, the camera at arm's length, and I didn't stop or care how blurred the images would be. I suppose it was the equivalent of looking in a mirror.

Money and a pearl necklace were missing from Step's jewellery box, and of course I was to blame. I was left in no doubt. I never bothered to tell them the truth, Step, Sam, mum, my step-dad. It was a lot of money too, apparently. Even better. It's something I can live with. *And* I'm painting again.

The Mirror

Any sketch she started turned into a sketch of a dragon. A faint outline drawn on the corner of a paper bag would split quickly into two or three massive heads that, despite their repeated appearance, always managed to shock her and slow her down, so that without looking up she was aware of the kitchen's every detail and the movements of anyone who might have wandered near. Then she would very patiently mark out the dragon's scales. She was good at this and at depicting a malevolent violence in the eyes. They were the dragon's eyes, not hers (her own were impassive).

She was drawing happily or unhappily as the café filled up. The Fair Exchange was something of an enigma as a name, had been ever since the paintings of fairground scenes were superseded on the walls. She had heard the phrase in a song being played on the workmen's radio while the white dust was doing its last rounds. Her ex-boyfriend agreed, and his mother, the owner, plunged into the mystery of a sudden change of name. When the girl looked resolute, she never crossed her.

The radio was playing again, and it hardly distracted her, not just because she was busy with the drawing but because there were no words on any track to remind her of herself. It wasn't simply self-absorption: it was just that, at this hour – and the huge kitchen clock said it was one – she was floating free of all consoling images of herself. Feeling this way, she walked out into the glare of the counter.

No, it wasn't so busy as all that, and Rachel – or Sophie, was it? – seemed to be doing all right; just all right. One of the two men still waiting at the counter to be served turned to look at her, while the other, nervous and fidgety, moved his hands like a butcher's over an apron, rubbing sweat off. She looked harder at this man, as if to intimidate him into turning his head also, then noticed that the first hadn't looked away. He had been in before, once, three days ago, and had sat underneath the painting of the upturned tree (or that was what she saw in it). She watched him – served by Rachel or Sophie – go back to that corner.

Was his name Tamas, Thomas even? It would be worse than a bad omen if it were. She had opened her *Bhagavad Gita* that morning and let her eyes select randomly the two passages for the day. For a while it was just one passage, then she discovered that she needed a second – to protect her from, say, being directed to buckle her armour and go off to war. Recently her interpretations had grown eccentric. Now it was superstition that gripped her. 'Darkness, inertia, negligence, delusion – these appear when Tamas prevails,' she was warned at breakfast.

Sophie had just come into the café, her name badge already pinned on, so the other girl was definitely Rachel. Staff flowed through this place like water. Only Stephen and his mother, out of all of them, had drunk champagne with her on that first night two years ago – contravening licensing regulations, but no matter. Rachel was itching to leave after only a fortnight, the signs were all there. She felt a moment's compassion for this hare-eyed girl.

'Rachel,' she said, 'leave that. You can take your lunch break now.'

'I'll work through, if that's all right,' Rachel was saying, 'and maybe leave an hour early, at three – if it's all right.' She seemed to want to discuss something, her plans for tonight perhaps, but she was cut short.

'Then I'll go.'

She buttoned up her coat in the entranceway and looked out on the street. If she were being true to form, she would walk now up the street of Georgian B&Bs – she loved one in particular that had the evocative name 'Lavengro' – draw out some money from the autoteller and buy a pastry she could have eaten for free in the café. Instead she stared at a poster she herself had put up – some student production – which annoyed her intensely. It dated back to the café's early days. She pulled it from the wall, surprised how easily and softly it tore.

The direction she took wouldn't bring her to a bakery or sandwich shop but did eventually broaden out to the Meadows. She could walk down one of the long avenues of trees – it was what she needed. She had walked that way one morning a year or so ago, with mist catching the back of her throat. She knew that she wouldn't be solitary now, but she was unprepared for the vast number of bodies spread out over the grass. Students, she thought, with the memory of the poster compounding her disgust. She sat next to a child on a bench and watched one group. They were saying things in false voices, laughing, then somebody would clap, somebody scream, and always something physical occurred, semi-disguised simulations of love-making or sad arm-wrestles. She wanted them to catch her staring, but they were oblivious. Everyone was, even this playless child by her side.

She still had a half-hour to kill. She was about to go back the way she came when she saw a coffee stand some way off, near the swing park. It was painted interestingly, 'fairground colours' she thought. Close to, she couldn't see any sign of coffee being sold; there were two men adjusting an engine at its side. She imagined that she felt some heat from the engine as she half-lingered there, until one of the men caught sight of her. He might have been picking food from his teeth, but it looked to her that he was sucking a finger suggestively. She couldn't believe that she was watching this.

If it had happened in the café she would have known how to react, she wouldn't simply have gone off like a frightened child. She was too angry with herself and with the man to be made angrier by the cavorting, laughing bodies now. She reached the edge of the park before the single thought going through her head was complete. Suddenly she noticed where she was. The good thing about her anger was that she had more time now.

Why shouldn't she do something crazy? There was the pub with the dark interior she had noticed that last time. She wanted to sit at a bar with a long face and drink, but habit, when she got beyond the squeaking door, restrained her. She carried her half-pint of Guinness to a table opposite the bar.

Nobody was in she need bother about. She wanted to isolate herself in this place with what she could hear and see and the contents of the glass and her hand holding it, feeling the blackness of the drink outside her like a blanket, a cape even, over her shoulders. She tried her childhood trick of not thinking, thinking about not thinking, abandoned that and tried to think coherently, actually in sentences, examining the last two years and always coming back to the image of Stephen and his mother. His attitude was easily defined, but hers? 'As though there were some man,' she thought carefully, 'whom she (Stephen's mother) wanted to seduce, and she (herself) was the man's daughter, whose approval mattered most to him.' As for Stephen – she had become his elder sister.

Why should that dismay her now? She had worked hard to achieve it. For an age, it seemed, she had sacrificed the new life she might have had away from him, from them – from circumstances she knew would ensnare her. She had grown abstract. She could stand a foot away from a body she had once clawed at in bed, and it was like standing in a steady drizzle of rain. It was even pleasant, like rain.

She was careful not to return the glass to the bar as she left. She'd be late now, but it didn't matter. Mints from the dank little newsagent next to the café was all she needed to stop for, though she did stop too for an additional breath, before pushing open the café door.

Sophie looked cross and Rachel was inside making noise in the kitchen. The ladies from the B&Bs had got as far as the corner of the street once again, she thought. There was no sign of either the awkward man or Tamas. Her shift wasn't over till seven. A long day. Sophie could scowl all she liked.

'Turn it up, when you're passing. This one's my favourite,' Rachel emerged to say. With Stephen's mother gone, they weren't restricted to playing ambient, elevator music.

'Brian serenaded me with this song outside the hostel one night, it was *so* funny. He says it's about me.' The other two smiled conspiratorially, until Sophie remembered her anger.

> She wears an Egyptian red ring
> That sparkles before she speaks.
> She wears an Egyptian red ring
> That sparkles before she speaks.

She was the only one left smiling, but to her surprise the words affected her, as though she had heard them before in a dream. She needed to get away already. 'I'll be in the back,' she said, not waiting for the spasm to cross Sophie's face.

The constant electric humming of the office/store, coupled with the dry atmosphere, was as oppressive as human company. She rested her cheek on a page of the open ledger, breathing in the foul paper smell, and squinted up at a photograph of standing stones, then the calendar (the number seven was circled in red ink), and her own spidery handwriting in a note to Stephen; passing from the handwriting to the words themselves – something about keys – she felt nauseated by the passionless tone.

Sophie walked in, as abruptly as the heavy iron door allowed, and stared down at her, at the pained expression – it was like animal pain – of this enemy of moments before.

'You all right?'

' ... No.'

'What's wrong?'

'I don't ... '

'You want to go home? We can manage here till Stephen comes.'

'I'm sure.'

'Look, I meant to show you this. I think that handsome guy that was in the corner when I came in left it. He must have meant you.'

She finally lifted her head and regarded the

scrawled note Sophie held out. The note seemed to puzzle her. *I'm going after you,* it said. *I think I know where you'll be. But if I don't find you, call me on this number – 668 1682. My name's Jordan, incidentally.*

'It was inside the empty CD case. It might *not* have been him, but I saw him near there ... Do you think you'll phone?'

'No.'

'Well, anyway, I'll leave you here. Just come through when you like.'

'Thanks, Soph. Soph ... '

'What?'

'I feel all right. Okay?'

• • • • • • • • • • • • • • • • •

After five minutes she felt resuscitated, more alive than before, and was pouring a customer her first coffee of the day. The three girls were together behind the counter, needlessly, jockeying for position to be the first to serve whoever came in next, imitating the sound of the espresso machine. Rachel felt bold enough to point to a dollop of spilled cream dispersing in a pool of water and say, 'What does that remind you of?' They all laughed and touched each other's arms, but only Rachel blushed. They were aware of disapproving heads turning towards them.

'Oh no,' Rachel whispered. They knew this customer for sure – Stephen King they called him. He was the one who sat for hours with two, sometimes three coffees, filling in various notepads which he spread out over a table six people could get round. He wore a hooded top and at times when he looked most intense he would put up the hood. Their only break from him was when he went outside for a cigarette. They sometimes wondered what he wrote, but they suspected that it was no good. 'A filter coffee, please. Thanks,' and 'Another filter coffee, please. Thanks,' was all he said.

Actually he made no impact on their high spirits, and

when his first cigarette break came round he left unobserved.

'How long's Stephen King been gone?'

'I never noticed,' Sophie said. Rachel shrugged.

She ducked under the end of the counter and walked to his table. 'I always wanted to do this,' she said.

She picked up notepad after notepad and the pages he had torn out of them, unearthing a large, slim book – *Modigliani* – which had been set face down on the table, concealing a nude Jeanne Hebuterne. She held it up for the girls' scrutiny and laughter. Then she sat down and read to where he had left off.

'You can't *do* that,' Rachel said. Sophie laughed, but worriedly, looking towards the door.

'He's angry with someone. Some girl. Can you believe this? He says here at the end "I *invented* you".'

'*Please*,' Rachel said.

'I seriously think you *should* stop. He's bound to walk in.'

When she took up his pen they almost howled with fright. She was writing something in air a few millimetres above the page, but she couldn't go through with it.

No, I can, she thought. She moved back round to the counter, lifted the hatch and went into the kitchen. Sophie, quick to appreciate this mood swing, found her scribbling on a paper bag

'I think I'll take you up on your offer. Stephen will be in soon, right?'

'Soonish.'

'I'll make it up to you, promise.'

She was putting her arms into the sleeves of her coat as she stepped outside. Two streets down and around the corner there was a phone-box next to a church. She found some change in her bag and looked at the note. There was no significance for her in the numbers ...

It only took that. She wished now that she had given herself more time to prepare. Did she need anything? Alcohol, perhaps, but he had said he would bring something.

No, she wasn't waiting on him now; actually she never had.

She was almost there, and walking up the stairs she noticed the close for what seemed like the first time. It wasn't so inviting. That *was* the smell of urine and there were layers of paint peeling off so that you couldn't say definitively which was the last colour. As if he'd mind, she thought. She thought, 'How do I know? I don't know him.'

Closing the door and walking through the rooms, she looked at the place through his eyes. What would he make of her? She was excessively neat in one corner and chaotic in the next (not randomly, she knew: the objects that were icons for her – a small vase depicting a heron in flight, that had a chip like a V-neck; the framed Klee print, *Ravaged Land*; the photograph of a tree trunk with a dark hollowed space that let light, and the background landscape, through: there were others – commanded a space around them, a neat space, gradually falling off into chaos again). Would he even notice?

She was sipping at a glass mug of green tea, calming herself, when the intercom buzzed.

She pressed the button and listened at the door.

He was better-looking than she remembered, and he had the grace to kiss her cheek without speaking, without hesitating. His coat, the same coat, was draped over one shoulder, and he threw it onto an arm of the sofa, revealing a bottle of Absolut. She lit an incense cone and put on some music. He had been speaking for almost a minute, clear, liquid words, and now he was filling two tumblers with the drink. She didn't tell him to stop: she wasn't worried, she hoped it would go to her head.

There was an exchange of names, unnecessary on his part, and an explanation of the note. He had been into the café more than twice, but it had been busier before, and she mightn't have noticed him in the crowd – or she mightn't have noticed him full stop. ('That's not possible,' she smiled.) He asked her why she had changed her lunch routine today.

'I don't impart that sort of information.'

'You don't?'

'No, I don't.'

She started to undress him even now. He misunderstood her turning away when they kissed – it was to bring the glass to her mouth and gulp more vodka – and that happened each time, as if he were caught in a loop of time. Time didn't exist for her: desire existed. It was a year since the last man, strictly speaking, and time had only flowed back to her, then, on the next morning, when she had crossed the Meadows in mist. She was licking even into his armpits. If he hadn't remembered to grin he might have lost himself.

It was a year, and another six months, since Stephen. This was the best, though. It kept on going and going and the only thing she wanted was to look in the mirror. She could drag him, still inside her, into the white, white bedroom, and watch their love-making in the solid wall of mirrors. She could do that ... She laughed – at the poverty of the one mirror she possessed, on the cabinet in the bathroom.

She liked what she saw. Liked? Loathed, loved. She'd left him behind, to scrawl out his second, final note to her – not that it mattered. He gathered his things, leaving her the Absolut and the note. In the bathroom she was struggling to remember the second passage from the *Gita*. She wanted to have it word-perfect in her head. Wiping the sick from her lips, she could nevertheless discern, without irony, something godlike in her appearance just at this moment.

Something godlike.

'How difficult thou art to see! But I see thee: as fire, as the sun, blinding, incomprehensible.'

Then Mona Says

It's so cold in the kitchen. Kay is on the stairs, waving her arms like she's flagging somebody home. She'll have to watch that mug of tea at her feet. One pink sock, one purplish blue. You could never say. I have to prepare my escape via some other route. 'Excuse me, have you seen my necessary appendage? I think it's on the stairwell, if I could just squeeze ...' No, it's not so gruesome, truly. I can stand to watch her left toes curl (pink sock), curl *down*wards, so that her foot arches. She's moving it around slowly, making little pockets of dust. Hand on a banister of air (where's that from?). I'll sit here, two more cigarettes. Contemplate this postcard cathedral.

Julie's good, acting like she can't act, doing wolf-howl yawns when Kay's attention strays. Reminds me of in the honey-coloured room, sprawled on her bed saying when she spoke, *My eardrums were popping*. She likes to be heard, I found that out. They'd make nice sisters though. Photogenic.

Someone's missing (someone's *always* missing), and that's Mona. Ask me why we call her that, I couldn't say. If she ever smiled seductively it was into a fridge, in my opinion. It was a toss-up between Mona and Bibbles, but someone fatter got the Bibbles tag. Someone not much fatter. I don't care. She has more curves than angles but she has a beautiful voice. Makes me think of medicine I took as a kid.

Not that we're sitting around waiting for her beautiful voice to arrive. Julie is conducting an anatomy lesson since she perked up, lifting her hairy top to below her breasts and squeezing skin, with both hands. She says she has too much of it, but I say, in a meaningful way, *No, you can't have too much skin.* Kay's pleading with her to stop, pleading-laughing of course, and soon we're all three exposing ourselves and laughing insanely. Kay's skin is a beautiful colour, Julie's is nice too. Mine's shrivelled lemon peel next to theirs.

Tell me again, Kay is saying through tears. *Tell me your apple strudel dream again. Oh tell me* ***please****.* I get up and walk into the alcove, where nothing is. Stupid. *Don't tease him,* Julie's saying – not in a way I'd thank her for – *don't because he takes his dreams* ***seriously****.* It's the last time I become personal with them. I'd like it better if they analysed you to death. Kay begins to pretend to, saying *Apple strudel, it's like a man on the outside and a woman on the inside, wouldn't you say?* I'm out of the alcove and scraping dead putty off a tile. They can't focus on anything longer than three minutes. They prove me right too. Julie's touching her toes and mentions Mona.

The girl's a sink, she says, *the more you put into her the fuller she gets.—Explain that,* we both say. I say, *It could be any vessel, or any****thing****, everything gets fuller.* She comes over all lucid and sparkling and says, *I mean it, you give her information and she can't sift it, after a while she simply* ***explodes****. Like yesterday. I was showing her salsa and she was chalking round my feet. I said to her 'Mona, watch. Learn. Then trust your instinct.' She said, 'Instinct I don't trust.' That says everything, don't you think?*

I could listen to her all day, though, I say in her defence. I'm looking for the word 'mellifluous' but I blush before I find it. Julie's cross, jealous. I speak about how fat Mona is, to calm things. Then *they* come to her defence and suddenly I'm a pig. Kay is on the back of the couch draped round Julie nearly and I'm still a pig. I notice the cold again, put the fire up to ignition, and they shout, *Put that down.* This time they keep up hating me, four, five minutes. I'm happy with that. Keeps them off my dream.

The door goes and Julie says, *Mona rings twice.* Then we wait. *That's not Mona,* she says, and *Did you pay the rent?* Of course I paid the rent. Opening the door would be a good idea, but I'm not the nearest, and besides I feel sort of paralysed. Kay is agile after a sigh and unlocks herself from

Julie. The back of her top has a million wrinkles. Then I remember she must have slept in it. She could keep her wardrobe here – might as well.

The someone not Mona at the door is Karl. Kay shouts it and I hear him take off his boots in the hall. I'm not slow to tell him: *You're supposed to be in India,* and he grins embarrassed and explains. It's too detailed. In addition, his feet smell, and Julie's discreet but even she opens the window full. That of course makes everywhere ten times colder. I'm about to give in, give up the ghost, but Karl's remembered something and Kay walks him out. Relief. Karl's not bad but nobody remembers whose friend he is.

I like Karl, Julie lies now he's gone. It's retaliation for my Mona comment, about her voice. I let it go. Kay is on all-fours between Julie and me, arching her back with her face almost on the floor, creature-like. She knows stretches. I feel like walking into the alcove again, but I have a cigarette, think about Karl and his boots and try to imagine India.

Karl bores me, Kay says, *going to far-flung places, doing wilder and wilder things because he's desperate and can't connect with anyone. It's why he's always breaking arms and legs. He bores me.* I'm respectful suddenly and Julie is too. Kay spoils the effect, though, as ever, cavorting across the rug like she's playing twister.

He's adventurous at least, Julie says lamely, still retaliating. *Do you like Karl?* (This to me.) *Do you?*

*I **adore** him.*

This works and they let me laugh along. After a while Julie looks at Kay, says *Why are there no animals in this place? We would be good with animals,* and I say *They're too civilizing an influence.* It doesn't get the big laugh I expect. *You read that somewhere,* Julie says. *It would be cruel to keep animals,* Kay says, *we could be moving out of here any day, or get dispersed.* I mention that we've been here three years. *Yes,* Kay says, *but any day now – you never know.*

Next, Kay's swinging a bottle through the air,

brandishing would be the word, a big squarish tequila bottle. *Want to join me on the stoop? Drink tequila?* She's talking in imitation of a Canadian boyfriend she had for about a day, someone we liked just as much as Karl. I don't know that she means it. She clarifies things: she *is* offering us a drink. Offering us *our* drink. *Is this your week for not drinking?* she asks. *No, but it's early,* I say. Julie's guzzling it, high drama of course, but I see her let most of it back into the bottle. *There's a drink in South America,* she says, *and they keep a scorpion in the bottle.* We both say, *No, there's not,* and she says *No there's not. I made that up.* She laughs. She drinks and I think she really is drinking. It means I will be cooking, for three. I don't mind.

That's Mona this time, Kay and Julie say. It's all right, I compose myself spectacularly, drinking tequila while they're in the hall. I know it's Mona too, but I begin to doubt it when I hear them speak. It's Mona, though, with a sandpaper voice, looking like she has pneumonia. New-Mona-ia. It's not funny enough to say. She greets me by not changing her face at all. I stand up and she slides behind me into my chair. She's a little breathless, as always, and moving her head around to take everything in. There's maybe another layer of mess for her to take in.

Has anyone moved since yesterday? Mona asks.

We've moved, I say. Kay and Julie agree. We're indignant, adamant that we've moved.

No, I mean outside?

We were just about to go out on the stoop. Drink tequila.

At three o'clock in the afternoon?

Since when were you everybody's conscience? Julie says.

I've come back from the police station, she says, possibly in answer. She lets it hang in the air. We're meant to be open-mouthed.

Why were you in the police station, Mona? I say to her, speaking like she's a four-year-old.

I was walking in the park, she says. *Up a slope. I stopped to catch my breath and I saw something glittering in the stream. I went and picked it up and it was a huge knife. Not a kitchen knife. I dropped it back down, but I started getting paranoid because my prints were on it. So I wrapped it in a plastic bag and took it to the police. I just got back.*

Why not bring it here? I hate the police, Kay says.

I didn't want to implicate you. Anyway it was me that found it.

Is that the end of the story? I ask.

No, it's not, she says. We all groan, first me, then Kay, then Julie.

It was pandemonium in the station. I had to sign a statement because apparently there's been another race riot in the Academy and someone got stabbed. There were schoolkids all over the shop.

Her voice is just about gone, and suddenly it's dead in the room and we're groaning quietly for real.

Mona, Kay says, *we're here enjoying ourselves, and you come in and it's like –* ***doom****. Please apologize.* Kay's back on the stairs, picking between her toes, the purple sock off.

Is that ***black*** *nail varnish?* Julie asks.

Then Mona says, *I don't believe you people. You know there's a world out there,* and lists the people who populate it. She mentions lawyers, policemen, social workers, teachers, architects.

She can't sift, Julie says, blowing a smoke ring towards the ceiling. Mona doesn't hear.

... ambulancemen, doctors, landlords, weathermen

Weathermen is too much.

Please stop, Mona, Kay says. *Mona,* ***please****?*

You three are growing together like ivy, Mona says next.

That's not an unpleasant image, I say.

It is unpleasant. I'm going. Outside? You've heard of there.

Mona gets up and moves her head again. We don't

walk her out. Not that we're rooted to the spot.

• • • • • • • • • • • • • • • • •

There is a world, Mona, I've seen it. There's a world inside, too, in these rooms, where Julie gets angry with me, and Kay spells every letter of the alphabet across the floor. I'm watching it, three years now, and it's sad, I admit, that I don't seem to know the first thing about it yet.

Dear Mona.

Devotion

Ada ran a finger along the mantelpiece and was satisfied. You couldn't ask a man to belittle himself by dusting: she had never asked that of Hugh, certainly. And where was he? He should have been here a quarter of an hour ago. Not that, in truth, his company was vital for the few things she needed, but she liked having a man beside her at the stop.

She decided that she must get Bea out of bed. It was normally safe to leave her, but a groggy Bea rousing herself and stumbling about the room was an unpleasant image, and, since Bea hadn't yet paid the bathroom a visit, this was all too likely to happen. She had failed earlier with a cup of tea, now she would swing Bea's legs out and fasten a hand under her right armpit and heave. And she would be right to scold Bea – Bea who was five years her junior, after all! – and warn that next time Hugh would be doing the lifting. 'You wouldn't *dare* allow him into my room,' Bea would say. 'Into *our* room, dear,' she would answer.

There was a rustling sound at the door and by the time she had investigated and discovered the polythene charity bag on the mat, it was too late to call after the deliverer, to tell her that this was the second such delivery in a week. She heard the main door bang, its hollow reverberations echoing through the stairwell, and then she heard Hugh's footsteps. He took the stairs two at a time, composing himself with a more dignified progression as he neared the sisters' door. Ada was resettling the chairback on the broad armchair.

'It's me,' Hugh's voice boomed out from the hall. He soon found Ada in the sitting room, panting slightly, with a *Family Circle* on her lap. 'Your door's wide open – Bea still inside, I hope?'

'You're late,' Ada said, not looking up.

'Speaking of the door. Before I forget ...' He was feeling inside his coat, unbuttoning a pocket of his boiler suit. 'They *had* the tartan nameplates in that shop. Just the surname. Best not to advertise that you are two ladies living alone.'

'Is that the Lochiel tartan? I can't tell in this light.'

'I don't think so, Ada. I think they were all the same tartan, only in red and dark green. You like a dark green.'

'Yes, it's an improvement. Thank you, Hugh. I'm afraid there's no time to put it up.'

'Is Bea up?'

'No, not yet,' she sighed.

'Will you be getting her up?'

Ada nodded.

'Then I'll have this on in two shakes while you see to her.'

Ada, a little put-out not to be directing operations herself, softened when she saw Hugh's profile leaning into the door, and heard the commotion he made attaching the nameplate – it was loud enough to inform any curious neighbour that the sisters could still make their presence felt. Well, she had better see to her sister, after all; if the day came when Bea were to see no daylight hours ...

The light in the room was the colour of the curtains – dark red. Ada's bed jutted out from the middle of one wall; there was a dresser, a wardrobe, and finally Bea in a narrow, high bed, well tucked in, not turning to regard the familiar figure hurrying towards her. Her hair, patchy and stuck flat to her scalp, produced an odour that, once it was in her sister's determined nostrils, made the action of wheeling her out of bed more speedy.

'Now,' Ada said when she had Bea's feet zipped up in ankle boots. Bea was already making the jaw movements necessary to eat the bread and jam that would come later. Ada hoped Hugh would be discreet enough to close the door over and work from outside, while she protectively hustled Bea to the bathroom, as though Bea were a hostage she had rescued from sleep; in fact, he had finished the work, and the sisters were startled to see his bulky frame reflected in the bathroom mirror.

'Ladies,' he said, and stepped aside, satisfied with his moustache.

Bea was not so bad an invalid that Ada would have to stand over her; nevertheless, it took a good hour at least from the time she got up for Bea to steady herself, and if Ada waited this long it would cut a great swath out of her day. No: once Bea had been deposited in the armchair with a light breakfast, Ada would be free to go.

Hugh was displaying signs of restlessness, poking about (his head was now under the kitchen sink), whistling some tune from *Carousel.* 'That's the musical the school must be doing this year,' Ada thought. 'He wants me to make some comment.'

'Hugh,' she said later, handing him the manly shopping bag he had picked out for her to buy, 'what are the children performing for us this year? Not *Oliver* again, I hope.' They locked arms and he led her along the hall; from the hall carpet to the concrete of the landing she took an exaggerated step, like an astronaut's. It signalled her respect for the world outside.

'*Carousel,* Ada. I don't know how many times I've told that drama woman not to let them use confetti in rehearsals. It's a bugger to sweep up,' he said, forgetting for a moment that this was Ada, while she, imagining that she had squeezed his arm, allowed herself a thin smile.

'Bea will be all right,' he said.

'Yes, yes,' Ada said, 'certainly.'

'These stairs could do with a clean.'

'Oh Bea,' she thought.

• • • • • • • • • • • • • • • • •

Bea's food needs had been met, the tray taken from her and a travel rug put in its place; then Ada had left. Bea looked like a lucky snapshot of a baby, taken just after tears or mischief had subsided, and it seemed for a few moments that she would stay this way. But, like a baby, something distracted her: a tassel of the rug, inspected and then flicked. With surprising strength, she tossed the rug to the floor, and began chuckling. Only the laughter wasn't babylike.

Something on the wall to her right caught her attention and then mesmerized her. Suddenly she put all her weight (it wasn't much) onto her right arm and the right arm of the chair and raised herself. It took several attempts, but she managed it, swaying a little finally, but standing quite tall. A few shuffled steps and she was at the mantelpiece, holding on with both hands. She seemed safe enough, yet her legs buckled slightly, and she threatened her own safety by passing her right foot behind her left, twice. She moved along the mantelpiece, to see better the little framed picture of Greyfriar's Bobby, or else the kirbie grip Ada used in her ears. She felt bolder now. Turning her head to take in half the room, she mapped out a route to the cabinet opposite: it would involve resting at three points, which were the two arms of the sofa and an arm of the armchair used only by Hugh. She passed all three successfully. Then, with real skill, without holding onto anything, she knelt down beside the cabinet doors; adjusted herself; opened one door and rummaged inside. She stopped as though mesmerized once more, and tried to look back over her shoulder, but it was less easy in this position. She returned half-heartedly to her search, taking out an old newspaper, putting it back, taking it out again. Then she closed the cabinet door. She was a good five minutes on her knees still.

She got to her feet with obvious frailty, but once she was walking she moved smoothly, as though battery-operated, into the kitchen. She headed straight for the long cupboard next to the sink. One thing inside it interested her: an old battered Quality Street tin, which she rested between her belly and a shelf and looked into. Replacing the lid, she made the same automaton-shuffle back to the sitting room, back to the armchair she had set off from originally. A drop of moisture from her nose hit the tin. With her right index finger she spread it out a little, looking intently at her work.

No expression passed over her face, but once or twice her eyes did clear, then darkened again.

• • • • • • • • • • • • • • • • •

Trestle tinsel tassie tassel. Ah yes. Horrible colours. What's that one? Purple? Bish bosh. Bish. Bosh. Tucked me snugly in, she says. She says. There – and good riddance to it. How about that?

I'm not sprightly, first thing, thinks I've not got it in me. Mother'd tell her. 'Beatrice is not what you'd call an early bird.' 'Beatrice never was a good riser.' 'Beatrice this.' 'Beatrice.' And no wonder, the way she claws at me. Can't wait to be out and about with her fancy man. Imagine. *Him* a fancy man.

Where is my Danny? He should be in that frame, it was a present to *me*. Now what's she got in it?

Steady. Use the arm. Now. One, two, three, *four*. Look at me, Ada, *look* at me. I'll lean on the – what is it again?

Mantelpiece. Yes, yes, I was a dancer, we did this, look. *And. Again*. Ada, I'm curtseying. *One* and ... and ... It's a little ugly dog. What on earth? What else has she put?

Disgusting.

Now. Look at the way she has the furniture round the room. Like a Home. But ... they make a good stepping stones. If I can just. Steady. Steady on my pins. Look at that brute of a chair. There. If I can *ease*. Ah, pause for breath. We filled our lungs, head back, *and*. What must they look like now? Those girls ... These lungs.

Are they sliding doors? This one opens out, silly. I'll have to, move ... back. There. Look at the mess. Like finding a needle. Where's she hidden him? There's one somewhere, the three of us, outside the ... Rep, it was. One at the Golf Club. There was Milly, that's right, she'd lovely legs. She put one leg in front of the other for the camera. And Peter, lanky Peter. What became of Peter? 'I could strangle you,' he used to say. To Milly. 'I could strangle you.' And an ugly fat lady.

Greyfriar's Bobby! That's who the dog is. That's right. I wept and wept. What a story! Sitting by his master's grave. He followed the coffin. The men from the pub fed him ... What are these papers? Keeping papers, she'll have him in some tin. No he's not here. Close it over again.

I haven't the. No, I do, once I'm on my ... It's a short sprint. *Through* the double doors, *through* the kitchen door, *sink* straight ahead, cupboard *right*. Once I'm on my. Steady. Steady on my pins ...

What about that now! Steady. Stop for breath. Oh it's chilly in here, better not stay here. Now. The long press. If he's not here, it's that she's ... Thrown him out. Oh, spiteful Ada, jealous, spiteful Ada. Never had a boy such as Danny. *Never*.

In this tin? Look at the mess. Wants me to prick myself. Watch for razor blades, that's her favourite. Well, I can't tell, there's so much. It's chilly. Bring it back with me. But if I fall ... Steady. Couldn't put my hands to support me. Oh these hands would snap like twigs. Quick now. Careful now.

Oh did she see that! Like a dancer! So swift. 'Oh Bea.' But I could use that thing now, that shawl if it is. If I can stretch ... to reach. No. Never mind, open the tin. These numb thumbs. Prise it, yes. No. But I did it before, I did it before.

There. Stop weeping. Stop ... now.

Look at that, a teardrop, landed on the tin. What was this, a sweetie tin? That's right. Landed on the beautiful lady. Such a lady. Nice material, look at that now, all bunched up, round her ... Quite the dashing sergeant, he. Or private. Who can tell? Just like Danny, you'd swear it. Stripes and ... epaulettes. Going for a stroll. Promenade. Past the little piers, little white piers. Brahms, I should think. Dainty lady. 'Evening.' Who are these other people? No no, it's the same two, that is amusing. Yes, quite beautiful.

No, better if there were just two, just the two, done once, nice and big, that would be lovely. No one else. No Ada, father. Not even mother. Not that father and mother ever.

No, Bea, be truthful, father also. Father and Ada and ... not mother. Mother approved. It was Ada, Ada, only Ada. 'I'm doing it for you, Bea. He's weak, weak.' 'I'm sending him away, Bea.' As if she could. She could never. Look at that now. Look at that lovely.

'He's weak, Bea, weak. I'm sending him away. You don't know the half, Bea ...' Jealous, little spiteful. 'Weak, weak.' She could never, she wouldn't ... *dare*.

• • • • • • • • • • • • • • • • •

Hugh had forgotten to buy rolling tobacco and was on the return path to the supermarket. Ada suspected his motives: she'd seen two of his pals standing at the automatic doors; so ignorant they were, they seemed not to realize that it was their own stilted movements which made the doors open and close repeatedly. She was left with the shopping bag at her feet, at the place in the bus stop where a queue ought to begin, but she was standing alone.

Ten minutes they had waited for a number eleven bus before Hugh remembered. If one came along now she would be tempted to get on. She *wouldn't* get on, but she'd be tempted. Hugh was in relaxed mood, enjoying his Friday half-day, and this returning her safely to the flat was a bind. He would only be back in the same spot an hour later anyway: the Stag's Head was on the corner of the road, which was where he started his weekends. Ada knew all about it.

Soon she heard laboured breathing and turned to see a red-faced young man beside her. He was dressed in grey jogging bottoms, black sweatshirt, and he had a sports bag propped awkwardly on one trainer. If he hadn't just escaped exercise then he was badly in need of some. Ada looked him up and down, but it wasn't her practice to initiate bus stop conversation: that was for other old people to do.

He was asking her about the number twenty-two, if it had been yet.

'Not in the last quarter of an hour, no,' she said.

'When is it due?'

'Every twenty minutes, but you know what they're like.'

He thought she had perhaps winked at him, or raised an eyebrow: something urged him to explain. He made the observation about buses all arriving at once.

'I'm sure bus-drivers are as industrious as anyone else these days,' she said, which made him laugh, perhaps mistakenly. 'Is yours a sedentary occupation?' She was pleased to see his quizzical look.

'An office job?' she explained. 'Something not too physical?'

He worked in computers, he said. He elaborated and she vaguely understood that he had asked a question. Looking at him, she had been lost in thought.

'You're not *from* here, are you? Are you English?'

Yes, he was from Huddersfield, he said. He asked was she local.

'And you moved here for work, did you?'

'Ostensibly,' he said. 'But for my girlfriend really, I suppose.'

Ada turned her head and looked to the left for a long time, as though watching for her bus, but of course it wouldn't come from that direction. The young man was puzzled.

'I'm waiting for somebody,' she said, turning back to him sharply.

He looked at the bag full of shopping and spoke about supermarkets; something about managing some account, she thought he said. 'But you can't beat the old corner shop,' he said ingratiatingly at one point.

'You believe that, do you?' she asked. 'I prefer supermarkets. They're so much more spacious, and cheaper, even for a few things. Have you ever thought of joining the Forces?'

He straightened up then, as if to attention, and tried to look this formidable old lady in the eye; but he found he couldn't and, visibly shivering as a result of his body cooling down now, he worried that this might look like fear.

'No,' he answered. 'Why do you ask?'

'It's a good way for a young man like yourself to see the world. That's all.'

He didn't realize it, but she had warmed to him, even as her voice continued in more and more clipped tones

The number twenty-two almost passed them by.

He looked at her and smiled quickly as the doors opened. She was annoyed that Hugh's approach disturbed the departure.

'Goodbye,' she said, in the awkward moment of him picking out his change from the plastic chute. 'I'll know you if I see you again.'

Jack's Version

'When all this is behind us we'll rearrange the furniture. I want rid of that German tankard she bought us for a start. Where are the white candles?' She caught a glimpse of herself in the round, rope-held mirror, an almost tall woman in her fifties in a black dress with a red poppy print. Despite the fact of her daughter-in-law leaning into the mirror's frame, she went on as if self-communing: 'In the brown-papered drawer in the chest of drawers, there's a couple there. Use them sparingly ... What's the youngest doing?'

'He's looking at the squirrels out the front window.' The girl's smile was transmitted to the woman she called Mum via the mirror. She had been slipping in and out of the dead woman's room barely noticed all morning.

'The candles aren't in that drawer,' she said the next time she returned.

'No? That old chest of drawers can go. Tomorrow we'll make a bonfire.'

'I'll do it, if you like.'

'Would you? That was always my job ... Look at you. I always wanted hair like yours – thick, black.'

They were busy preparing for the corpse to arrive. They had already removed everything from the bed, clearing a space for the coffin, and now the most visible traces of the grandmother's existence in the house were being expunged; not just shifted to other corners of the sprawling, two-storey, twice extended house – expunged.

'Really you'd need rubber gloves to go through this.' She emptied out the old hatbox onto a bleached spot on the pink carpet – the grandmother had grown very fond of bleach towards the end – with the smell of must nearly overwhelming her. The box had held a hoard of kirby grips, rubber bands, razor blades, dud batteries, even an ancient cigarette coupon, though the old woman had never smoked, and a once transparent and now opaque plastic statuette of

Our Lady, filled with Lourdes water. 'Make that boxing gloves,' she said, holding up one of the blades by a blunt edge for inspection, and then suddenly shooting out her free arm to bring down the girl fully, until they both were kneeling, both laughing exaggeratedly.

The moment was slow to progress to an embarrassed stage. Eighteen months before, the intimacy would have been impossible. The only concession the daughter-in-law made to her confused self of that time was the cheesecloth blouse she could never part with: away went the braids, the wasp-coloured socks, the jeans she would happily have written phone numbers on – and she did collect a few phone numbers back then. When she conceded defeat, when she failed to find a man to satisfy her other than this poppy-bedecked woman's son – when in fact she admitted to herself that he always had satisfied her – his willingness to marry her had not faded. That was last autumn.

'Mum,' she said, pale-faced, 'it's her.'

The woman joined the girl at the window and watched the emergence of the old, old lady's parting shot: the coffin returning to the house for the family to pray round, as, dying, she had insisted. It was a custom foreign to this street – a rebuke to her own irreligion, she knew.

'Be a darling and let the men in, will you? I'm almost finished here.' She wanted to hide a face of rage alone in the room.

• • • • • • • • • • • • • • • • •

The youngest son was frozen in a harlequin-like pose for only a few seconds, until his left hand brushed over his face and he came to life again and turned away from the dark men pointing a coffin towards the house. He leapt onto an arm of the orange sofa in imitation of the squirrels in the tree outside the window, but he didn't manage to make it across to the other arm in one go. It made him angry with himself.

Sitting cross-legged half underneath the folding dining table, he listened to the sounds of the invisible men as they seemed to crawl pounding their fists up the stairs, and guessed their location in his grandmother's room above, his eyes scanning the white ceiling: they stopped for four seconds at the Y-shaped crack before the final thud. His speculation faltered then: this was his second death, but the first that he would go on to remember. They were all involved in dark rituals, his mother, Sylvia and the three strange men, and beyond that he knew nothing. He couldn't decide if they were conspiring against him.

The door to the living room opened and his brother Michael walked in.

'Hello, Jack,' he said affectionately, 'the front door's lying wide open.' A spasm of understanding crossed his face and he looked out of the window. 'They upstairs?'

The boy – whose name wasn't really Jack, but who got called that by his favourite brother ever since he jumped like a jack-in-the-box out of the shoe cupboard playing hide-and-seek – nodded gravely. Michael fished a bag of wine gums out of his briefcase for him. Jack had only ever seen a bag of sweets that size in the cinema shop.

'I suppose I *should* go up,' Michael said in their old pretend manner, 'but to tell you the truth, grasshopper, I'm reluctant to. You don't mind if I hang around you a while?' He looked with dismay at the flesh-indentation between the boy's eyes, went to the kitchen and made himself a coffee, Jack all but tugging his trouser-legs for attention. 'There's nothing in here for you,' he said, closing the fridge. 'But plenty of water in the taps, sahib.'

Jack settled on the arm of the sofa and looked at the mysterious symbols turning rapidly in the air. Michael was flicking through a newspaper.

'I'll teach you how to read, if you like,' he said, bringing the paper back to its front page. 'That's an N, that's an M, and that's an E. *NME. New Musical Express*. So the first letters of your name would be, let's see, JB for Jack-in-the-box.' Jack's fist came down rapidly on the newspaper, into Michael's groin.

'What's up, grasshopper? That hurt.'

Jack abandoned the sofa and positioned himself instead far back in the wooden rocking-chair and stared at the TV. It was switched off.

'There's an article here about the new Zeppelin album that's coming out. That should fascinate you. No? You'd be a big hit with the girls in the playgroup if they thought you were a Zep freak. Jack?'

There were a few seconds of silence between them and then the steady progression of footsteps down the stairs and into the hall. The men were leaving. The two brothers waited for the living room door to open, their mother or Sylvia to appear, but the door stayed closed. They took up their silence again.

Now Jack was gently pouring some of the wine gums onto the seat of the chair, his legs splayed to accommodate them, and grouping the sweets according to colour. It was his plan to eat one from each pile, beginning with yellow and ending at black, but with the yellow, green, white and red in his mouth at once, he had to concentrate on chewing these down to a manageable pulp before continuing.

Michael re-read the article, this time out loud, some of his own interest and anticipation seeping into his voice. Depressed by the slowness of his eating game, Jack raised himself up by his arms, hovered over the wine gums and slid onto the floor. He stilled the rocking-chair and crept back over to the sofa.

'It's a good title, grasshopper; enigmatic.' Michael pointed to the page in awe. 'You want to know what it is? Jack, you want to know?'

Jack nodded.

'*Presence.*'

Jack looked up at his brother's mouth as the word was repeated, and not only mirrored but perfected the look of awe. Michael was impressed. But then he laughed hard at what Jack said next, starting again the whole cycle of resentment and silence, only worse this time, with Jack running out of the room.

'Presents,' Jack had said.

• • • • • • • • • • • • • • • • •

'I didn't know you were back. You're standing there exactly like Jack was before. I was looking for him.' Sylvia placed two fingers into each of his hip pockets and crooked her knees into the back of his legs.

'It's a long tradition in our family, staring out of the window.'

'Why didn't you come upstairs? The coffin's there.'

'I know. It's not going anywhere tonight, though, is it?'

'That's why I'm looking for Jack. He ran into the room and saw his gran lying there and ran out again. God knows what it did to him.'

'Better to let him see her,' he said.

'You think so? But not like that.'

'He's a tough kid.'

'We both know that's not true.' She kissed his neck, happy for him not to respond; bit gently into his collar before going on: 'You ought to see her, she really does look peaceful. We laughed at something. The undertakers had put make-up on her, really quite garish. Your mum said she never had make-up on in her life.'

'Did you take it off?'

'No, I couldn't, never. Oh my God.' She laughed again.

'I was thinking something a minute ago. He got upset when I called him Jack-in-the-box. I didn't think about it at the time. Do you think he saw the coffin coming in?'

'If he was still at the window. I looked everywhere upstairs. Stay here and I'll look in the kitchen.'

She left him staring dreamily into the boughs,

opening his mouth wide in a silent animal-like yawn to break the tension in his head – not only his head, but every part of his long-immobile body.

The kitchen was deserted, but Sylvia found the back door open: if he had gone through a gap in the hedge, she realized, he was probably next-door.

The next-door neighbour confirmed it, waving to her from the washing-line.

'He's inside with Alice, happy as Larry.'

The gap was broad enough to let Sylvia through sideways. The two women, one newly pregnant again, the other newly married, stood face to face and talked about death, then they talked about the two children. The neighbour wanted Sylvia to walk over the soil around the daffodils and look in on them through the kitchen window.

'They're making a mess with soap,' she said, 'but I never mind.'

Jack was elbow-high to the sink and he was winning. With his best friend Alice he was spinning a dark green bar of Fairy soap in his hands and producing more lather than Alice could with hers: he knew just when to dip his hands into the running water without washing the lather away. Their bright, still babyish-looking clothes, and the home-made wooden box that supported them and enabled them to play this game, were drenched with soapy water. Jack suddenly grew tired of his easy victory and dropped the soap. Alice looked on, puzzled. She had to stagger back onto the linoleum as he squatted abruptly down on the wet platform. He bunched his fingers into little fists and drummed on the wood dramatically.

'En-em-y,' he hissed, his eyes narrowing. 'En-em-y.'

The little girl was appalled. Just at the right moment, though, Jack dropped his drummer-boy persona, stood up smiling and walked towards her. She noticed the difference, and her face took on his ecstatic look. He stopped a few feet from her, saying 'Pres-ence' just once, before the faces appeared in the window.

After the Film

Now he watches for her coming. It will be after the adverts stop and he has just closed the doors, when the cinema is dark, that she'll appear. And the same words: 'It's all right, I don't need the torch.' Three times in the past seven days she's been, possibly more: she must know some of the dialogue by heart. He sits through *Last Night* every night, but for money. She has a reason too; must have.

It has got something to do with her cat. The cat was what he noticed first. Cats' eyes – unmistakable. The little dark head swivelling at the top of her coat, but not a sound, nothing, as though it were one of the drugged babies of beggar-refugees in the news now. That was when he should have asked her to leave. He was like a man who catches sight of a break-in and is too fascinated to tear himself away. Besides, he couldn't recall any regulation referring specifically to animals. Drink could be brought in from the bar in a plastic glass, so why not a cat inside a coat, especially when the wearer of the coat – his eyes, accustomed to cinema dark, could tell – was a woman this attractive?

His boss, a woman at least physically attractive, is snapping him out of his trance, saying: 'I think after seven years I deserve to take it easy.' He's missed what went before, and so she repeats herself huffily and he trots off to the box office where the queue is long and Jackie is getting snowed under. He curses his luck until he realizes what his luck is: the chance to catch her in broad daylight, catch her and, with a wink, perhaps, a knowing smile, something to alert her to him – to let her go.

There are five, six, seven customers before she appears wearing an overcoat that's clearly too big – but that's not her ruse. Her ruse is a simple shoulder-bag: she must transfer the cat, from the bag to inside her coat, in the cinema. He feels vaguely disappointed, as though he wishes she feigned pregnancy or smuggled the creature in under a Russian hat (she is wearing a headscarf). He tries to judge when she will get to the front of the queue, but the ticket-printer is slower than usual or else he misjudges. She is speaking to Jackie. Not a concession, she says – odd for a weekday matinée – takes the ticket and goes. He looks at Jackie, asking silently 'Did you see that? Did you notice anything?' Jackie stares back, says 'What?'

His boss returns when it's quiet again and takes over. 'I'm bored by that film,' she says. 'I thought it was supposed to be about the end of the world. There's not much action. Do you remember, Jackie, *Earthquake*, when they made the seats in the cinemas shake, and ... Why are you still here?' This is not so brutal as it sounds to him at first, and her body collapses slightly with amusement before she directs him with a different voice, one that's tender-firm, masking the brutality. He feels ashamed as he walks back to Screen Two – no, *pads* back, he thinks, pads like a gentle bear ...

It's got to the part where the guy sleeps with his old French teacher, one of the things he means to do before the world ends, and people are laughing. She is just two rows from the back. This is careless of her, he thinks, *if* she wants to avoid detection; if he features in her thoughts at all. Her head is quite pertly tilted up to the screen, as though she were seeing this for the first time. It makes it fresh for him.

When the film ends she sits through the credits, something she hasn't done before, so that once again he gets to see her clearly. She is also the last to leave. There isn't time for him to analyse these developments and he waits for her at the top of the stairs, tempted to place a friendly hand on her departing back. Either the desperate prospect of sitting through the film again – or one of the two other films showing, or whatever his boss has got planned for him – or else an odd, wrenching surge of courage, makes him say when she is in earshot: 'Can't your cat guess the end by now?'

'Cat?' she asks, reading his face. She responds to his placid, wilful smile, saying believably, 'But I didn't bring her today. Here, look through my bag.' She apologizes, seeing his embarrassment, then asks him how he knew. 'That's a dumb question,' she says, cross with herself. 'You saw her, right?'

'More than once. I take it you like *Last Night*?'

'I love the ending.'

'The world blowing up?'

'Not that.'

He finds that he is showing her to the front door, the two of them walking leisurely, but by the time they get there she still hasn't satisfied him about the cat. He asks her to meet him later, about eight.

'I'll see you here,' she says, 'here,' marking an invisible cross with her right foot.

• • • • • • • • • • • • • • • • •

'It's the one with the shutters closed, third floor. I'll be five minutes, tops. Come up.' He follows close behind on the tenement steps. There's something she has to see to at her friend's place, where she's 'sort of staying' and where he'll get to see the cat. There are around a dozen names on a scrap of paper on the door, all but three under the words MAIL FOR. He sees that her name isn't included. A girl with a towel round her head opens the door, looks at him unsmiling and says 'I'm in here,' as she leads the way. The way is into an enormous, drab room with what look like architectural drawings on the walls; there is a dart-board and a woman's dressing gown folded over a tailor's dummy in such a way that just one breast is showing. Left alone with the friend, he sits on the sofabed while she lies on the king-sized mattress on the floor. He lifts off a mug part-filled with cold coffee.

'You work at the Arthouse, don't you? I never go there. Where are you and Vicky off to tonight?'

'Some pub, I suppose. I've said a few places but she's a hard girl to pin down.'

'Girl?'

He is so used to this sort of frostiness today that he says nothing and lets his gaze bounce off the walls. 'You don't mind,' she says and turns the sound up on the TV; he reaches out to the short mantelpiece of books, takes down a book on self-harm and replaces it. There is a guide to Tantric sex, a biography of Peter Warlock. If Victoria and her cat are a mystery, then this girl (girl?) is another. He can't make her out.

The cat's sudden, sleepy appearance from a wardrobe takes the sting out of the moment. Stroked and called a he on the sofabed, she trots over to the circular rug in the room's centre and faces the TV. He thinks now that he can talk about the cat being in the cinema.

'She can't be left here all day if we're out. Is that where Vicky's been going, *every* day?'

He grows nervous, but he's brought it up now. 'More than once,' he says lamely.

'Vicky's not really supposed to be here, but we worked together when she was still working, and she needed a place to stay, and so she's here, and now she's invited you back. I'm sorry, but can I watch this? I don't mean to be rude.'

'Really, she doesn't,' Victoria says from the doorway. Her hair is down, beautiful, and she has a black tulle dress on, her arms open towards her friend inviting comment. 'I've borrowed these, and this,' she says. 'Come here, darling.' She holds the cat out from her body and leaves the room. He sits on until the friend says, 'I think you're going now.'

'Nice room.'

'This is Giorgio's room,' she says, still not looking round, 'he lets me watch his telly. Have a nice time.'

'She's nice, really,' Victoria says on the stairs. 'She disapproves of my lifestyle, sometimes. She's a bit frustrated – fancies one of the blokes she's living with, but he's a serial ... what's the word? Not adulterer.'

Out in the street he manages to ask what her

lifestyle is. She answers vaguely, uninterestedly, 'Oh you know, nothing really bad,' and he thinks he'll wait, it'll come out.

'Let's get a taxi,' she says. 'That white one.'

She wants to go somewhere expensive, tells him not to worry. 'I scrimp like mad during the day, but nights are different. That's why I like the cinema in the afternoon, it's cheap and warm and kills time. Problem is there's never much good on. You must hate *Last Night* by now.'

He quotes a line of dialogue but all she says is: 'Is that in the film?' He thinks this is her sense of humour.

Soon they stop at a place called Larry's and he pays the taxi. Inside, the light shows up the state of his clothes, which had been fine for work, but. Victoria looks not out of place. Eventually they sit at the bar: he covers up the problems he has with the barstool by saying, 'This is so light, like balsa,' while her laughter tinkles erotically. The barman is like someone from a film.

He wishes he knew what to ask for, but the golden taps are unidentified, and so he looks up and asks for a Jameson's. White wine for her. Even though he has just ordered, the barman shows him the drinks list. 'He's pointing out the prices,' he thinks.

'There's a seat at this end of the bar, sir, if you would like a table.' Victoria, taken in by the remark, thanks the waiter, not seeing that they are the worst seats, close to the door and screening them off from the other patrons. Which is probably what they are called here. He hates the rich.

'Never mind that,' she says, stroking his hand once, with one finger. It doesn't make everything all right, but he tries to let it; looking into her eyes helps. It is still too soon to probe for information.

'The premise is so simple,' he says, 'you think it must be a rotten film. It's really just a weird love story. When his parents wrap up old presents from the loft and act like it's Christmas, I couldn't stop laughing. It's the kind of thing I can imagine mine doing.'

'Some Christians lived like that,' she says. 'Early Christians. As though each day was their last. Consciously thought: "This is my last day on earth." I don't believe that could work. Reality is always different.'

'It was like that speaking to you today, I was thinking how nice it would be to speak to you when the film ended and then I spoke, but I was so flustered.'

'You were as cool as anything.'

'You think that?'

She grows quiet, lost in thought. 'What would you do if this was your last night on earth?' he asks. She smiles at him not quite deafly without answering. His drink is already finished.

'This place is vile,' she says, 'let's go somewhere cheap.'

'One more shot. I'll down it straight off if you like, but allow me. Incidentally,' he says, leaning back down, having just stood up, 'who does the barman remind me of?'

'I don't know. Let me pay for your shot.'

He calculates how well or badly things are going and feels the balance could be easy tipped. Not by a single false move, but by two or three. That line, 'What would you do if this were ... ' – he shouldn't have come out with it. She had been talking seriously, intelligently. What she had said ... He hopes she's not a Christian, at least not the born-again sort. (He knew one once, she had a lazy eye – it was her only moral failing, that eye's laziness.) Perhaps he can steer the conversation back to the film, or would it be harping too much on cinema, as though he had nothing else to him? How could he bring it up, or how would it sound? 'About last night ...'

She returns angry, picks up her coat and apologizes – she will buy him a drink in the next bar, the barman here is truly awful – and, as they leave, he casts what he thinks is a lingering look of hatred in the direction of the bar. But the barman is polishing a glass, smiling at a tuxedo.

She's happy to walk and wander into somewhere

nice, and at a certain point she takes his arm, in an old-fashioned way, but then lets it go. There might have been something he could have done. It's odd, walking down city streets with a woman on a summer night, not talking about the end of the world. Suddenly she speaks about herself, and unprompted tells him that she lives off a private income, 'like some Chekhov character'. 'I noticed you didn't ask for a concession,' he says. She shudders and says, 'I didn't see you there ... It's sort of creepy, the thought of being watched.' He has made at least his second false move.

'There are two pubs on this street, on either corner,' he says, thinking an anecdote will help. 'I went into that one with a friend one night and we got our drinks and sat down and I had this feeling of doom, I knew that something *terrible* was about to happen. I was so convincing we left and crossed the street into the other pub. I was fine and chatting when a bloody crate came through the window, *on my head*, and the glass down my back.'

'Sweetheart,' she says. 'Diddums.'

'I was all right, it was the premonition I was pointing out.'

They stop at the kerb and he feels it is hopeless. She's not touched him since. She's barely listening. If an intimation of occult power can't move her ... There is his friend, a different friend, from way back: he is on the other side of the street and waving.

He puts an arm round her to bring her near so that he can whisper – everything he can say in a few seconds about his friend – but her discomfort's plain. It sets him off on the wrong foot with Davey. Who's not alone, he sees now. There's a woman running up to him.

They all talk except for this woman, and Davey passes a bottle of red wine between them.

'Drinking in the street.'

'What's so wrong with that?'

Victoria asks what he was like young, and there's some laughter, but the talk degenerates, Davey saying to

Victoria: 'And now I bet he goes to church on Sundays.'

'Why are you saying that?' he says.

'He used to want to burn down churches. "Let's torch the church." Remember?'

'Davey, it was lovely to meet you, but you're starting to scare me now, so goodbye,' Victoria says and laughs, and they split into two couples again.

He thinks. *This is the end of everything.*

'How would it be if we forgot drinking? I feel different now,' she says.

'If you like. Do you want me to walk you ... ?'

She walks him into a narrow street, and a narrower one, which opens onto a small square with backs of offices round about. There are fire escapes going up the buildings.

'The first one,' she says. 'First floor.'

'Where are we going?' he asks, a genuinely plaintive tone to his voice.

She looks at him, equally puzzled. 'Where? This is my home.'

'I thought you lived ... '

When she closes the door she says, 'Temporarily. I was supposed to have moved out of here a month ago. We'll have to hide if the landlord comes round, on the floor. He doesn't have the new key.' The room they are in, he now sees, has boxes, a hamper, a wooden crate and a disconnected phone; also some blankets. 'I owe him money. You know, I'm not rich. Most of my stuff is stored in the other flat, but sometimes I sleep here.'

There is a noise on the stairs which passes. They are on the floor, just about containing themselves. Then they roll together.

'What would you do if this was our *first* night?' she says.

The Prince

He was a colleague – but that's too harsh a word – at a young offenders' institution out in the moors somewhere-nowhere, and back then he was quite a prince. His whole body vibrated perceptibly, like the bass-string of a guitar, in tune with his spirit. When it comes to 'spirit' I am an atheist normally, but you had to see this guy. He liked to wear a large speckled crew-neck jumper that made him look like a Swedish fisherman, plus his hair was spiky; sometimes his pupils were so big with excitement you'd think the irises were black as well: his gaze didn't pierce you so much as drink you in. So was I drunk in, many times, before we spoke. The occasion was his wonder at my name, Marlon. At a staff training day, after we'd caught the miniature bean-bag that was thrown between us all and said who we were, we broke for coffee and he sidled out of the room with me, saying 'Marlon' as if it were in italics in his head; then he said it again, with a question-mark. I explained about my name, and other things, even got onto the subject of my parents, when alarm bells rang: nobody, in my experience, took this kind of interest except a teacher, one that wants to be your 'friend', and I was a long time out of school.

I accepted his own name, Robert, simply, to show that it could be done, not asking if this was his paternal grandfather's name or should I call him Bob. At lunch-time I found that he was still with me, and in order to shake him off I invited him back to Isabel's room: Isabel could eat ten Roberts for breakfast. She was in her Japanese dressing gown, and I winked at her when I saw the window wide open and incense burning. 'Smoking this early in the day,' I said to her, pretty sure Robert wouldn't know what I meant. Isabel was in fact disappointingly subdued, whether because of the dope or the stomach cramps she complained of I couldn't tell. I tried goading her with observations made to Robert, such as my favourite, that she had the look of an animal:

which animal in particular was in doubt – a hyena, perhaps? He grew uncomfortable, of course, but differently from how I'd intended, more out of sympathy for someone victimized. Claire helped me save face when she came in demanding an introduction. She was up for goading Isabel too, making a fuss over me as I lay back on the bed. 'I think Robert's getting excited,' she said, looking at him while she stroked the insides of my thighs. Red-faced though he was, he showed some mettle by making us all laugh then. 'This?' he said. 'No, this's just a small pencil I carry round with me.'

From inauspicious beginnings, it turned out to be a memorable day. There was an afternoon more of the mind-numbing banality of staff training, a grotesque canteen dinner, then the four of us got re-acquainted in the nearest village pub – the 'nearest' anything meaning quite a hike away. Robert was drunk after his second cider and I had to play out of my skin for us to beat the sullen locals at pool. Claire and Isabel cheer-led from the sides, but predictably their support wavered: I looked around to see who it was that interested them. My Swedish fisherman drank himself sober, and he was a good companion once we were holed up in our usual booth. Isabel had decided to be my girlfriend again.

She was whispering to me fondly and so on just as Robert got into full conversational flood. Even the girls had to admit he was impressive like that, his sentences running on into the gulps from his glass. Claire spoke as if he wasn't there, saying 'I don't know what to make of him,' and for long stretches that night you couldn't have said exactly *where* he was. He expounded his philosophy of life so unsatisfactorily that he had to reach out for a beermat, irritably rip a layer off, and write out a quotation from Wittgenstein's *On Certainty* (I know: I still have the beermat; he included a footnote). We were adrift in a sea of abstruse talk. I found myself licking peanut salt from my hands just to get a sensation of something real. If only he could be shrunk, I fantasized, and put on a mantelpiece and kept at home, my mother would love him. He had wound down by last orders and we had the problem of how to get him moving outside. By the time we left I knew which of the tall strangers the girls had eyed up earlier: it was from his direction that we heard the words, so full of sour grapes, 'Night night, *Marilyn*.' Robert raised his sunken head to the level of a bull about to charge. We caught him and swung him out the door, letting him mutter and stagger the whole road back.

My instinct, though I liked Robert, was to keep him at arm's length for a while. I doubt if he even noticed. Claire and Isabel ensured that he was always around somewhere, Claire attaching herself to him in the corridors and canteen, with Isabel, so far as I could make out, treating him as though he were an addition to her collection of dolls. But if he was an unspoken preoccupation of mine at that stage, he didn't remain so. My ears pricked up in work at Eleanor's mention of his name. Eleanor was the new staff on the team and no gossip. I was so amused by her rage at Robert's transformation at the hands of my two girlfriends that I forgot to defend their honour. I told her that Robert was my friend, and if she ever wanted to meet up with us ... She responded, to my surprise, with great calm, saying 'Yes, all right, as long as it's only the two of you.'

It would be disingenuous of me to say that I didn't want to play the gooseberry, when that's exactly what I wanted. I sat and watched the awkward mating rituals in pub after pub; strolled between the two of them through cool glades or wherever we happened to be. Eleanor hacked away at him until his awkwardness and intensity resurfaced, and there was no sight more thrilling to me than that of Robert then, as he attempted to choke back the warble of embarrassment in his voice while telling us why we shouldn't commit suicide straightaway. It was Eleanor who teased him and suggested each new subject. I found the whole thing stimulating. Claire and Isabel all but disappeared from my evenings, though we bumped into them now and again in some pub or other, on nights when

I'd have the double pleasure of seeing the girls bed themselves into new and dangerous company and observing the lovebirds at my table.

Eleanor was soon bold enough to do without me. Once I realized the game was up, and I was being dropped from their plans most nights, I gave the pair my blessing and moved on. Isabel welcomed me back, though I had to share her now; Claire was always away. I used old newspapers to help me recall the weeks just past, and wrote up a detailed diary. Events in the Gulf War were a good source. On February 23rd, for instance, Eleanor had slipped her hand into Robert's for the first time, and for this day I quoted General O'Neill's words: 'I think we have a good feeling. It's been intensive and the results are bearing fruit.' I culled that from the *Times*. Of course I still saw Eleanor at work, and I visited Robert in his room as if he were any old friend: we told each other jokes we'd heard from the boys that day or just listened to music. I got bone weary of my loneliness after a while and gradually reworked the block's timetable until Eleanor found herself alone in my company on those quiet last half-hours of her shift. Soon there was a special atmosphere about them: I could tell that she felt it too. I don't know why, but sitting with her in the office, speaking about my parents' divorce and so on, I began to make up stories about my past, stories about old girlfriends – one had Munchausen's Syndrome by Proxy and poisoned her little sister, that sort of thing. She listened with some of Robert's wide-eyed intensity until I couldn't stand it, and then I would tell her to go. But she wouldn't leave early, no matter how quiet it was.

An evening came when I left her no choice. She had struggled through the day with flu and by night-time her face was so white she looked leprous. Come ten o'clock I didn't fancy being too close to her in that shoe-box of an office. I insisted she leave; I had to have the internal phone in my hand, ready to call for emergency cover, before she relented. I put it back down when she left. This was a mistake, a simple one, but a mistake. The screams came just as the first of the night staff walked in, so that, continuing her momentum, Mrs Porterfield was the first at the boy's bedside: even this minor point would count against me. I looked at the blood on the pillow with disbelief. Why now? Why in this one half-hour? The boy who'd given his room-mate a sore face, with some wire he'd unhooked from his bedsprings, was standing like Boo Radley behind the door. I coaxed him out, remembering my training, but I couldn't help myself, and had him pinned and squealing on the floor. I must have dragged him a little way across the room then, considering the carpet burns that showed up when he was examined later. Mrs Porterfield called the medical block and saw the rest of the boys back to their rooms. She made a mug of sweet tea for me.

My crime was to have broken the golden rule, of having enough staff on duty to cope. If Eleanor had stayed and listened to me spin a few more tales the same incident would have happened but we would be blameless. I could have said I had patrolled the corridor every ten minutes, as we were obliged to do. My roughness with the boy might have been overlooked at least in the Incident Report. I kept Eleanor out of trouble, but she was so well thought of that no one was really gunning for her. I must have pissed somebody off, because a month's suspension followed for me, and an internal investigation into the block. If I kept my head down, I knew, stayed on site – visible, but not too visible – nothing would stick. I could even do with the holiday.

I hadn't reckoned on Robert. Whenever Eleanor sent him away from her sickbed he'd scurry round to my rooms to dilate on injustice. He carried versions of events between us until the story was seamless and it was apparent that we were – I was – unquestionably the injured party. A red mist descended over those wide, black eyes. It turned an unpragmatic philosopher into a warrior on my behalf. I heard more gossip in a few days than ever in my life, from the stream of visitors: Robert's tirades in the kitchens, the TV rooms, even the snooker room, brought my way. I could have broken a few hearts with the information I possessed.

I let it go too far, though. Soon Robert was raising my case in the staff training sessions I was also suspended from. As I heard it, he had begun by speaking about a hypothetical situation: that was Robert all right, I thought. The trainer, one of the management team, pulled the rug from under him when he said 'You're referring to Marlon, I take it.' Perhaps it was the frankness of these words, or the laughter which followed them, but something breathed fire into Robert's belly. A part of me was sorry I missed what came next; all of me knew that the upset he caused would rebound on me and on him. In under a week I had word I'd be starting at a new block: not a demotion, but working with the least able, most bloody-minded inmates. It was how they edged people out.

Robert didn't need to be pushed, and when he spoke to management it was at his own request. At that meeting – but on impulse, I believed – he resigned. He'd got to be such a pain that his month's notice was waived. I was so numb that I couldn't tell yet if I would miss him. Incredibly, he seemed to think that I would jump ship too, but I remembered that this was his first job and he didn't know better. He might have more success persuading Eleanor, but it was doubtful that she would leave with him: their romance was barely off the ground and she was a conscientious sort of person. It wasn't a surprise to me, then, when she arrived late one night at my door. I let her in and we talked for about an hour and she left. I saw that distress really pulled her apart; exhaustion gave her an almost relaxed look, but not like the composure she was so good at summoning when needed: more a kind of languor. I was studying her and hardly noticed what I said: an ironic speech, I imagine now, about following your heart. Whatever, it worked. The next time I saw her she brought Robert along, and they both looked shiningly happy. They were leaving that night, Robert legitimately, Eleanor without a word to anyone. It would have been ruthless to argue against it, to put a stop to those enormous grins.

They accepted my offer to cook them their last meal; in fact they hung about my rooms until it was done. I knew that Robert was playing the songs he felt meant something to me, but I found this sentimental, ingratiating even, and I didn't respond. Eleanor, crushing garlic on a saucer in the space next to me while Robert changed the music once more, suddenly kissed me on the cheek. 'I think your mother named you after the Brando of *Guys'n'Dolls*,' she said, 'not *Streetcar* at all. You're a sweetheart, really. You have a voice like Brando's too, no wonder you won't sing.' In the end they had to bolt down their food and get a taxi to the airport to pick up the hired van. Eleanor's dream of leaving unobserved didn't happen, and the snooker room crowd helped to load up. It was all made less easy by the snow, April snow, which continued to fall. There was still some light in the sky when their white van crawled out of the grounds finally. Four of us showered snowballs on its roof.

I didn't hear from them again for another six months, but perhaps it took them some of that time just to track me down. I worked a fortnight on the new block, and then my month's notice. I'd no inclination to follow them north. I found work in a small care-in-the-community house in Brighton: my references were all sound. It was easy work, if you discounted the boredom and repetition. There *was* someone there I half-heartedly went after, but she was less easy to impress than most, or I had lost my touch. I had lost my share in Isabel, now that she was engaged, but still heard from Claire: Claire had left to become an aromatherapist. It was Robert who initiated our correspondence. The amusing postscripts to his letters were Eleanor's work, and she'd even underline her name with a smile, but Robert could never hide his feelings. I mentioned in one letter that I'd be alone at New Year and Eleanor wrote to invite me up.

They lived next to a disused railway line; after

studying the *A to Z*, I decided that taking this route would be an easy way to find the place. Besides, it was sunny: *cold* sunshine, but good to walk in. Their tenement block was the only one in the street made from red stone, and their door, three flights up, the only door in the block without a nameplate: Robert opened it.

Not much about his appearance had changed. It looked like he still cut his own hair, and he was wearing that same jumper. Eleanor was in the kitchen putting the final touches to a cold lunch. Her face seemed drawn, pinched-looking, and her clothes were new and different, more expensive. She talked all through lunch as though her life depended on it, and that was how I noticed the change in Robert: his silence. It was a defeated face I sat opposite.

Eleanor had the evening's activities mapped out. We were going to the carnival, then back for nibbles and some drinks, and then there was a choice of videos to bring us up to the bells. The 'carnival' was an assembly of fairground rides and hamburger stalls set inside a giant warehouse. None of the rides brought colour into Robert's cheeks, and when he was sent away like a child on some pretext or other, Eleanor spilled out her troubles. She wanted me to speak to him, not tonight, but one afternoon when she was at work. It seemed that Robert had nothing to fill his days, except perhaps fantasies of revenge involving our old management. She looked at me sidelong and unconvinced, and said: 'Even if he had a hobby ... Marlon, I've never lived with a man before, I feel like I'm not doing it properly.'

They were words which made me almost hate Robert. I used the next two days to size him up, work out my approach, but the vacant stare that met mine told me all I needed to know: people like Robert couldn't be helped, they could only be destroyed, then perhaps they'd have a chance of rising self-renewed from the ashes. 'Let him self-destruct, destroying him isn't *my* job': the thought satisfied me until I was left to face a long afternoon in his company, knowing I had to find *some* words. 'You used to talk for hours about the need to be silent,' I said, 'and now you're silent when people need you to talk.' He was shaking slightly, but I doubted that I was responsible. The tautness of his spirit, which had once made his body quiver, was nowadays simple nervousness – the shakes. I recalled to him the days of his former glory. The memory of our philosophical discussions late into the night – punctuated by obscene jokes and music – flooded me and made me bolder. I tried to tell him what I had learned and how I saw his own situation, fixed by rage as he was in one period of time. I acknowledged my own inglorious present, but pointed out to him what was good in it. This got mixed up with other, melancholy thoughts. 'When you're young,' I said, 'you *are* the music, then you get older and the house is empty, silent, and you wish you'd even learned to play a musical instrument, wish you knew how to play the piano so that you could at least play a tune that'd help you *remember* what you felt.' A twitch of his face, his hand rising to his lips ... something summoned the old Robert for me, for a few seconds. No, longer than that, because now *he* was speaking, steadily and passionately, though with his body still slumped in the chair. 'And that's your attitude to what's happened, is it? Everything between us? It's all aftermath with you, a perpetual hereafter, like a married couple picking out some evening class they can go to together – yes, *piano* lessons – because their love's failed.'

'It's only your opinion that it's failed,' I said. Whether this made sense or not, it ended our afternoon. I walked the streets until I knew Eleanor would be back, and the next morning, saying nothing to her eager face except 'Goodbye', I left.

I was too stubborn to keep in touch, but Eleanor wouldn't let our friendships die, phoning and writing until I agreed to visit again. So it went on, Easter, a week in summer, the whole of one Christmas and New Year. Robert got slowly better, but neither of us hoped for the Robert we'd fallen in love with to return intact. I stopped trying to create dramas wherever I went and began to enjoy life. Then one night, this New Year in fact, after Robert had gone to bed feeling listless, Eleanor and I sat up talking and I said it was just like those half-hour chats we used to have at the end of a shift.

'That's right,' she said. 'You used to tell me stories – those awful old girlfriends of yours. I loved listening to your lies. What an imagination!'

Embarrassed, I looked away, but felt able suddenly to ask the thing I always avoided.

'Do you ever think of leaving him?'

'No. I've made my choice. I always knew it wouldn't be an easy ride with Robert ... Remember that night I came round to yours, wanting to know if I should leave with him? You were so cynical back then. I would have stayed with you if you'd asked. You didn't know that? It's all many moons ago now ...'